DA
WATERS

MW00918075

A San Juan Islands Mystery:
Book Two

**The Writer
**Dark Waters
**Murder on Matia
**Rosario's Revenge
**Roche Harbor Rogue
**Turn Point Massacre

To my daughter Sienna.
P.S., I love you…

There is pleasure in the pathless woods, there is rapture in the lonely shore, there is society where none intrudes, by the deep sea, and music in its roar; I love not Man the less, but Nature more.

—Lord Byron

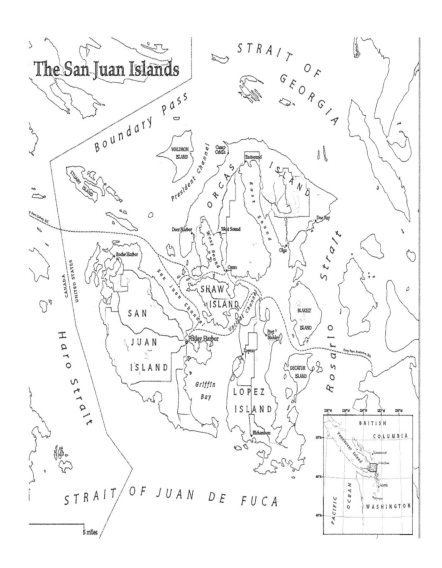

The San Juan Islands

STRAIT OF GEORGIA

Boundary Pass

WALDRON ISLAND

Camp Orkila

Eastsound

President Channel

ORCAS ISLAND

East Sound

Deer Harbor

West Sound

Orcas

Doe Bay

Olga

Roche Harbor

San Juan Channel

SHAW ISLAND

Upright Channel

BLAKELY ISLAND

SAN JUAN ISLAND

Friday Harbor

Port Stanley

Lopez

Rosario Strait

CANADA
UNITED STATES

Haro Strait

Griffin Bay

DECATUR ISLAND

LOPEZ ISLAND

Richardson

STRAIT OF JUAN DE FUCA

5 miles

BRITISH COLUMBIA

Vancouver Island

PACIFIC OCEAN

WASHINGTON

PROLOGUE

They are always hungry. *Metacarcinus magister*, more commonly known as the Dungeness crab, the bottom-feeding crustacean horde that populates much of the underwater world of the Pacific Northwest.

Some have called them nature's garbage collectors, feeding off the unwanted, the forgotten, the too soon or too long dead. A gathered mass of these little creatures of the mud and sand can rip the flesh off an entire human body within mere days, leaving nothing behind but sea-bleached bones. With claws and mouths at work, what once was will be no more. Whatever consumable thing finds its way from the surface to the seafloor below, the crab will seek out and devour.

Such is their unquestioning nature.

So it has been for millennia, and so it was on the night the remnants of a hacked and torn shell of a woman's body were stuffed into the narrow, metallic confines of a commercial crab pot before being hastily dropped into the dark waters of the San Juan Islands. The pot, overflowing with its grisly contents, swiftly made the 170-foot journey to the awaiting saltwater tomb below, and within minutes the Dungeness pack moved as one toward the flesh and blood scent that was carried upon the collaborative backs of both tide and current.

The young woman was just nineteen years old when a conflagration of happenstance led to her murder. She was deemed an inconvenient threat, and so her death meant very little to those committed to her ultimate undoing.

The ending of her life was merely a precaution, a territorial act carried out in secret with only the unblinking eye of a full moon as witness.

Or so they thought.

1.

Early summer:

"Focus, Adele. Remember, don't hit *at* it, hit *through* it."

Adele Plank's right hand protested the effort. Her scuffed and reddened knuckles gave off a dull thumping pain. Just the act of making a fist caused her to wince. She adjusted her shoulder-length, chestnut-colored ponytail and glared at the half-inch-thick wooden board that appeared to be silently mocking her failed attempts.

I can't do it. I'm not strong enough.

Thirty-six-year-old Robert Frank, known to his students as Sensei Rob, tried once again to push out Adele's seemingly constant self-doubt. He stood wearing the loose-fitting all-white dobok that was the formal attire for practitioners of tae kwon do. Adele was dressed much the same, with one critical difference. Sensei Rob's belt was black, whereas Adele's remained frustratingly blue.

"There is no pain, only your action and the universe's reaction."

Adele relaxed her newly lean five-foot-four-inch frame, closed her eyes, took a deep breath, and then reopened them to find the unblemished board staring back at her. She never imagined a simple piece of wood would possess the power to intimidate her so much.

Sensei Rob's dark-brown eyes implored her to throw the punch. It was the final test before the Bellingham University martial arts instructor could elevate her to the next level and award her a purple belt. Over the previous six months, Adele had taken to her training with an intensity rarely seen from beginning students, and Sensei Rob did his best to teach her as much as both her body and spirit would tolerate.

Another punch was thrown.

Adele cried out as her fist rebounded off the board's unyielding surface and then did her best to fight off tears. She wanted to cry, not so much from the pain but from the failure and the terrible unknown such failure represented after having just recently graduated with a degree in journalism.

She had no idea what to do with the rest of her life.

There were job offers in places like Seattle, Portland, Denver, and San Francisco, but Adele had started to wonder if life in the proverbial big city, the very thing she had once dreamed of, would in fact prove a terrible mistake.

Adele was emotionally adrift, uncertain, and increasingly confused. She had for so long prided herself on being a person with a plan but now found that plan no longer fit her newly formed self. Having already experienced some measure of success the previous year with her article on the remarkable reunion of Decklan and Calista Stone, Adele discovered aspects of that success in some ways left her feeling even more empty and uncertain. She didn't merely want to write about life; she actually wanted to live it.

What good is experience if it isn't your own?

"How about we take a break and revisit the test next week?"

Adele's eyes widened slightly as she realized her mind had taken her to a place far removed from the upper-level gymnasium within the university's expansive athletic complex. Sensei Rob lowered the board and gave her a reassuring smile. The son of Vietnamese immigrants was just slightly taller than his student and had a lean, athletic build; long-fingered hands; a narrow face; and dark, short-cropped hair. When he moved, he always seemed to be bouncing slightly, as if gravity was barely able to contain his boundless energy.

"I'm sorry, Sensei, I really thought I was ready."

The tae kwon do instructor shook his head.

"It's not about ready or not ready, Adele. You've already proven yourself a very capable and determined student. Your technique, your sparring performance, you've made considerable progress. It *will* happen, but it cannot be forced. You certainly have nothing to feel bad about. Everyone is different. Each of us learns and moves at a pace suitable for our own unique needs at any given moment in our lives."

Sensei Rob gave his student a quick bow, and then Adele did the same, signaling the formal conclusion to that day's lesson. She watched as he disappeared into the hallway outside the gym entrance and then let out a long, frustrated sigh.

Alone again.

Adele had become all too familiar with the sense of loneliness since her graduation. Her love life was nonexistent, and with no more university classes to attend, her once-familiar daily routine was seemingly absent of purpose or direction. She was even considering applying to graduate school to pursue a master's degree. Not so much because she actually wanted to, but so she could still remain safely cocooned within the world of academia, where growing up was no more a requirement than growing old.

"Hello there."

Adele whirled around to see a most unexpected surprise.

Decklan Stone stood no more than twenty feet away smiling at her. His greeting was the same two words he had spoken to her when they first met on his private island just over a year ago. He was dressed in a pair of tan khaki slacks and a white T-shirt. Despite the casual attire, he still somehow managed to appear every inch the dignified novelist.

"Decklan! What are you doing here?"

The writer shrugged and then moved forward to give Adele a quick hug.

"I had some business to attend to in Bellingham, legal odds and ends, and thought I'd try and see you before heading back to the islands."

Adele's smile was likely wider than she intended so great was her surprise and happiness at seeing the author standing in front of her.

"How'd you find me?"

"Ah, just a bit of investigative research on my part, I suppose. I tried to call you first and when there was no answer contacted your former newspaper editor, Mr. Levine, and he informed me you were spending a good deal of time here learning how to fight crime, leap tall buildings, or something of that nature."

Adele noted how his nearly sixty years were finally catching up to him. Gray had all but overtaken much of the hair on the sides of his head, and the lines that extended beyond the corners of his eyes had deepened considerably. And yet, those accumulated years only further added to the writer's natural mystique, a quality he carried with him far more easily than lesser men who expended so much effort trying to appear and act younger than they actually were.

He's still one fine-looking man.

Decklan peered up at the gym's high ceiling and then took a moment to notice the difference in Adele's appearance.

"You've lost weight! Not that you were heavy before, but you're definitely a leaner version of your previous self. It seems this fighting stuff suits you, Ms. Plank. You look wonderful. I wish Calista could be here to see. She sends her regards, of course."

Adele was grateful for the compliment while also wondering why Decklan had gone to so much trouble to find her. The question caused her to feel the initial stirrings of worry.

"I'm so happy to see you, but why are you *really* here, Decklan?"

"Ah, I am but a messenger. It seems our mutual friend, Delroy, had an offer he wanted to make to you but requested I wait until after your graduation to do so. He didn't wish to have an undue influence on your potential future plans."

The mention of Delroy Hicks, a man who had died of cancer months earlier after helping Adele solve the mystery of Decklan Stone's long-missing wife, left her even more confused.

"Delroy? I don't understand."

Decklan's brow lifted slightly as he tilted his head.

"As you well know, Delroy had an often unique perspective on life, the world, and our place in it."

The remark made Adele smile as she realized how much she missed Delroy's particular brand of wisdom. He had been, as Decklan just described, a truly unique individual.

"But what does this have to do with me?"

Decklan was about to answer and then abruptly stopped as he further pondered the question.

"Have you had lunch yet? I'm rather hungry. It'll be my treat. Calista and I missed your graduation, so I owe you at least that. Take me somewhere you consider your favorite place to enjoy a meal. There, we can discuss the specifics of Delroy's offer to you."

The word *offer* piqued Adele's interest even more. Decklan's sudden and unexpected appearance was shrouded in mystery, and a mystery was something she found impossible to resist.

Adele abruptly nodded her head.

"Let me change and then meet me out front. I can drive if that's OK."

Decklan shrugged.

"That's fine. I took a cab here from the airport."

Minutes later found Adele driving Decklan in her used MINI through a myriad of neighborhood side roads. It was the first time the writer had seen so much of Bellingham. The city had a certain awkward charm to it, like a somewhat uncertain adolescent who showed great promise but hadn't quite yet achieved it.

Adele arrived at the waterside neighborhood of Fairhaven, where Decklan was surprised to find himself feeling right at home. A red cobblestone street ran through the center of the community, dominated by multistoried red-bricked buildings on either side, some of which were more than a century old. Adele parked in front of one of those buildings and then pointed to a sign that hung from the corner. It read, "The Lost Cat".

"This place has a great view and the most wonderful crepes you've ever tasted."

Decklan hadn't realized he was smiling until he caught his reflection in a storefront window.

"It's very much like the San Juan Islands here. Perhaps a somewhat more cultured version of Friday Harbor."

Adele was quick to indicate her agreement.

"Exactly!"

Soon, Decklan was following the recent college graduate up a flight of steps that led to the restaurant's arched third-floor entrance. The smell of freshly prepared food made both their mouths water. An attractive dark-haired woman dressed in a form-fitting black dress greeted them with a smile.

"Welcome to the Lost Cat. Would you like the dining room or the bar?"

Adele indicated they would prefer a window table in the dining room. Once seated, Decklan stared out through the aged single-pane glass at the Fairhaven shoreline, Bellingham Bay, and the dark outline of the San Juan Islands beyond.

They both ordered coffee and two servings of shrimp-stuffed crepes. After taking an initial sip from his cup and finding the brew more than satisfactory, Decklan leaned back in his chair and folded his hands on the table in front of him.

"Let me start by letting you know Calista and I will be leaving soon, and we'll likely be gone for some time, perhaps as long as a year or more."

"Where are you going?"

Decklan took another drink from his coffee cup and then cleared his throat.

"Initially we intend to stay in New York to visit with family. We promised we would do so when both our physical rehabilitation programs were complete."

Adele's eyes widened as she suddenly realized the slurred speech that had plagued Decklan after his earlier attempted suicide by drowning was all but gone.

"I'm so sorry! I hadn't even noticed how much better your speech is! You're just like your old self!"

Decklan's gaze momentarily lowered. He was both pleased and slightly embarrassed by the compliment.

"Thank you. It's been a lot of work, but, yes, I'm very nearly back to the way I was before, well, before I did what I did."

Though the physical impact of having tried to kill himself was all but gone from Decklan, the shame of that act clearly remained.

"And Calista is still doing well?"

Decklan's face instantly brightened.

"Oh, yes, she's doing wonderfully. Every so often she'll have a bad dream involving her time in that cellar, but other than that, she's the woman I knew and the woman I hope to continue knowing for as long I am allowed to do so."

Decklan Stone glowed with the all too rare light of the truly content man. He seemingly had it all: health, success, and the remarkably resilient love of an equally remarkable and resilient woman.

The crepes arrived, filling the table with their delicate aroma. Decklan was first to take a bite. He chewed slowly, closed his eyes, and grinned.

"Yes indeed, this is very, very good, Adele - just what I needed."

Adele took a quick bite from her own plate and then continued the conversation.

"Are you going somewhere after New York?"

Decklan wiped his mouth with a linen napkin as he nodded.

"Yes, we're going to spend several months traveling Europe. Some time in London, Dublin, Paris, and then a month or so at a seaside villa just outside Marseilles."

Adele reached across the table and gave Decklan's hand a gentle squeeze.

"I'm so happy to hear you and Calista are doing well, Decklan. Lord knows you both deserve it."

Decklan had another sip of coffee.

"Don't think I'm not aware how much it kills you to have another potential mystery laid out before you, Adele. You've shown a remarkable bit of patience up to this point."

Adele's eyes narrowed as she realized how much Decklan enjoyed drawing out the details of Delroy's mysterious offer.

"Stop torturing me, Decklan. What's this all about?"

Decklan folded his perfectly manicured hands in front of him as he leaned forward and stared into Adele's eyes.

"This is about a choice, Adele - your choice. Over the years, Delroy would sometimes tell me how one of the great tragedies of life, beyond its inherently brief nature, was the lack of choice too often absent to those living it. He wanted to ensure you were given a choice but one you are free to accept or refuse. That is why he arranged to have it offered to you after your graduation. And since that graduation has come and gone, here I am with your choice in hand."

Decklan's right hand opened up to reveal a single age-worn key.

"Here, take it."

Adele did as she was told, surprised at how heavy the little key was as it came to rest in the palm of her hand. She was more confused than ever.

"Decklan, what choice are you talking about?"

The sound of laughter filtered into the dining room from the bar area as someone finished telling a joke.

Decklan's eyes remained fixed upon Adele's, holding her captive in his stare.

"The choice of the life you wish to live and the person you hope to be, Adele. That key represents a potential home for you, a life unfettered by monetary obligation, giving you something of remarkable value: both the time and the freedom to discover who you truly are and the path you were meant to take."

Adele stared down at the dull bit of metal and watched as the light from one of the restaurant's ceiling lamps was absorbed into it, making it appear as if the key was winking at her, a gesture that reminded her so very much of the man who had bestowed upon her this strange gift of potentially life-altering choice long after his own life had ended.

What the hell are you up to, Delroy Hicks?

2.

Adele stood staring at the sailboat that occupied Slip 22 of the picturesque Roche Harbor marina while holding tightly to the key given to her by Decklan two days earlier. He had explained that the legal "odds and ends" that brought him to Bellingham had involved finalizing aspects of Delroy's last will and testament. Delroy had made his longtime friend the executor of his estate, and the only remaining bequest was the one the former college professor had left to Adele - his beloved on-the-water home.

Delroy was giving Adele a place to live, free from the obligations of a mortgage or rent. If she instead decided against making the sailboat her home, it would be sold and the proceeds given to various island charities specifically noted in Delroy's will.

As she continued to look at the boat, Adele replayed Decklan's final words to her before he boarded the single engine seaplane that would take him from Bellingham Bay and drop him off at the dock in front of his private island home in Deer Harbor.

"He left a letter for you inside the boat. He wrote it just a few days before he passed. It took him a good deal of time as he was barely strong enough to hold the pen by then. I offered to type it up for him while he spoke the words, but he insisted it should be from his own hand. That was Delroy, always doing things his way. Read the letter, think it over, and then make your decision. Take as long as you need to decide. In fact, I'd suggest you take the rest of the summer. Enjoy the islands, the water, and in the end, you do what's best for *you*."

Adele found herself unable to step onto the sailboat, knowing that doing so represented a decision that would likely have a lasting impact upon her future.

But Delroy's letter is inside, and I have to read it.

The early afternoon June sun mingled with the cool breeze that swept off the surface of the Roche Harbor waters. The docks were busy with summer traffic as hundreds of new visitors arrived daily to the resort. With a deep breath, Adele stepped onto the sailboat and then used the key to unlock the varnished wood door that led down into the vessel's living area.

The space was just as Adele remembered it minus Delroy's personal items, which had already been removed. A small sitting area was located opposite an equally small but functional kitchen, and toward the bow was a sleeping nook and bathroom. The place smelled of teak, polished brass, and memories. All that was left was a framed black-and-white photograph and a white envelope with Adele's name on it written in dark ink.

The photo was of Delroy and Adele sitting on a pair of lawn chairs in front of his sailboat. Delroy was laughing while Adele looked at him with an especially wide smile on her face. She recalled the moment perfectly. It was just days after they had discovered Calista and saved Decklan, and weeks removed from when Delroy was forced to spend his final days in a hospital bed as the cancer ate away at what little of him yet remained.

Adele found it remarkable that a man near death still had a laugh that remained so full of joy and love of life. She ran a hand over the glass surface of the framed picture and then used that same hand to wipe away tears.

If anyone knew how to truly live in the moment, it was Delroy Hicks.

The envelope remained in front of the photograph, beckoning Adele to reveal its contents. She picked it up, felt the weight of the paper inside, opened it, and began to read the words of her departed friend. In her mind, she heard Delroy's Irish-accented voice as if he sat no more than a few feet from her with his always-present fedora perched atop his mass of gray hair and eyes lit with self-satisfied mischief.

To my dear friend, Adele,

And so, you have made the journey to this home I have left for you should you choose to accept it as yours. She's both a sturdy and a noble craft, well suited for future adventure, much like yourself. Thank you again for giving me what was to be my final endeavor. We did well, did we not? You have a remarkably keen sense of observation, which allows you to see what so many others miss. It was that very quality that saved two lives and made them whole once again.

Don't ever forget it was *you* who accomplished that. Knowing you, however brief that time proved to be, brought me great joy and satisfaction, and I wish to pay you back for what you so selflessly gave to me—purpose. I saw the love you had for these islands. I know that look well, having carried it in my own eyes and heart for so many years. It is a fortunate thing to find a place that feels like home even before one thinks to make it so.

This particular corner of the world would be well served by your insight, your compassion, your intellect, and, ultimately, your humanity. That said, if you choose to share your talents with a different part of the world, please, by all means, do so. This offer is not meant to confine you to these islands but rather to welcome you to them.

Summers here are both beautiful and boisterous, with the hustle and bustle of the high season and the thousands of visitors who accompany those months. Winter is a more contemplative affair but no less interesting with its accompaniment of storms and seeming solitude from the world of others.

Should you decide to make this your new home, there is a lovely couple in Friday Harbor you should not hesitate to introduce yourself to. Their names are Avery and Bess Jenkins. Find the old two-story green building overlooking the ferry terminal on Warbass Way. You'll locate them on the first floor facing the water. Just look for the Island Gazette sign above the door. Tell them your name and that I was the one who sent you, and then let potential opportunity take its course.

As you well know, this is a place surrounded by dark waters beneath which hide the potential for great mysteries both old and new. You have an especially unique knack for solving such mystery, and it gives me great joy to be able to offer that potential to you now. I'll be watching.

—Delroy

Adele stared at the letter for several seconds and then returned it to its place in front of the framed photograph. The sailboat rocked gently from side to side in its slip as a series of waves created by a vessel leaving the marina massaged its hull.

It was the middle of the week, early afternoon. She had plenty of time to make the short drive to Friday Harbor and meet with Avery and Bess Jenkins. That thought made Adele shake her head and smile as she realized Delroy had managed to dangle a mystery right in front of her nose via a letter he wrote many months earlier. He knew she would have no choice but to find out more about Avery and Bess. Her insatiable curiosity demanded she do so.

It was settled. Adele would go to Friday Harbor.

She made her way outside and began to walk down the wooden dock when the voice of someone from her own San Juan Islands past abruptly halted Adele's progress.

"Ms. Plank."

Adele didn't want to turn around. The haughty voice still managed to intimidate her.

It was Tilda Ashland, longtime owner of the Roche Harbor Hotel that overlooked the entirety of the resort and marina, and the same Tilda Ashland who had previously proven such a difficult interview subject for Adele as she sought to solve the twenty-seven-year mystery of Calista Stone's disappearance.

"Hello, Ms. Ashland."

Tilda was dressed in a sleeveless, cream-colored dress that covered her from the neck to just below her knees. Her thick, red hair was tied in a ponytail that hung well below her shoulders. The older woman's eyes moved up and down slowly as she took in Adele's presence, and then the hotel owner did something quite unexpected.

She gave Adele a genuinely warm and welcoming smile.

"Are you here visiting?"

Adele was caught off guard by the friendly greeting from a woman she knew to be the emotional equivalent of an angry viper. Tilda sensed the younger woman's uncertainty and was quick to try to make amends.

"I know I didn't exactly give you the best impression when we met before, but that was in many ways a different time for all of us, was it not? I was certainly a different version of myself then. We thought Calista dead, I was convinced Decklan had played a part and that no one wanted to hold him to account for what he had done. That's all changed, thanks to you. I owe you an apology, Ms. Plank. It's why I came down here when I saw you arrive earlier. My conscience demanded I do so. You deserve at least that much."

Adele struggled to respond with little more than a guarded smile and nod of her head.

"Uh, thank you, Ms. Ashland."

"Please, call me Tilda. Can I offer you some lunch?"

Initially, Adele was going to refuse the offer, but then she instinctively reminded herself that Tilda Ashland represented decades of San Juan Islands knowledge, making her a valuable resource should that information someday be needed.

"Yes, thank you, but if I'm going to call you Tilda, then you should just call me Adele, OK?"

Tilda's eyes widened slightly, revealing a hint of surprise at having her offer accepted. Then she smiled and pointed toward the three-story white and green-trimmed Victorian hotel.

"Very good! Let's be on our way, then, *Adele.*"

Soon after, Adele was seated opposite Tilda at a small table on the private balcony that adjoined the hotel owner's third-floor personal residence. The location provided both women a vantage point from which nearly all activity within the multi-acre resort could be seen. Tilda filled the white-and-blue porcelain cup in front of Adele with freshly brewed jasmine tea. Adele took a sip.

"It's very good, thank you."

Two halves of a cucumber and cream cheese sandwich sat in the center of the table. Tilda took one half and nibbled on it while her eyes remained fixed upon her young guest. Adele took a bite from the other half and tried to ignore the fact she was being stared at so intensely.

"I'm sorry. I'm making you uncomfortable again. Old habit. It's just . . ."

Tilda's voice trailed off, and then Adele completed the thought.

"You're wondering what I'm doing back here. Specifically, why I was inside Delroy's boat."

Tilda took a deep breath and then nodded.

"That's *exactly* what I was wondering, though I won't require you tell me. After all, your business is your own."

Adele took another bite of her sandwich, using the time to chew and swallow to gather her thoughts before responding. She decided to tell Tilda the truth, at least some of it.

"Delroy left his boat to me in his will. I just learned of it two days ago from Decklan Stone."

Adele watched as Tilda looked out at the open waters just beyond the marina and wondered what the suddenly silent hotel owner was thinking. Finally, Tilda broke her silence with an admission that, though somewhat out of place, confirmed for Adele something she had already suspected was so.

"I loved Calista, you know, and resented Decklan for being the one she chose to love instead of me. Now I understand how selfish that was. How it gave me an excuse to lose myself within a prison of my own self-loathing. All those years I wasted never to return, washed away by the thoughtless tides of time."

"Do you still love her in that way?"

Tilda gazed at Adele with narrowed eyes.

"You are always seeking to know more, aren't you? I suppose that's a big reason why Delroy took to you so quickly. He, too, spent his life trying to answer the riddle within the riddle, piecing together the past so as to try and better understand the present. Do I still love her in that way? Perhaps, but it no longer matters. I am happy to once again be able to call both Calista and Decklan my friends. So tell me, Adele, where is it you were going before our paths crossed?"

Adele finished her sandwich, washing down that final bite with the last of her tea. Again, she decided it best to proceed with the truth.

"Delroy wanted me to look up Avery and Bess Jenkins. He said they would be expecting me."

"The owners of the local newspaper?"

Adele shrugged.

"Yeah, I guess. Do you know them?"

Tilda nodded.

"I know *of* them. Avery attempted to interview me following Calista's disappearance all those years ago, but I ran him off and told him never to come back. After that, I think he thought it best to avoid me altogether. As for Bess, she would entertain friends here at the resort from time to time, though I haven't seen her in years. They both must be well into their seventies by now. I recall them as seeming old to me when I was still a young woman, not much older than you are now, and that was, of course, quite some time ago. Do you need transportation to Friday Harbor?"

"No, I have my car here."

Tilda stood up and extended her right hand across the table.

"Safe travels, then. If I can be of any help to you, don't hesitate to ask."

Adele shook Tilda's hand, marveling at the woman's much-improved disposition compared to when they had first met last year, though she remained uncertain over whether she could trust that transition entirely.

"Thank you, Tilda. It's great to see you doing so much better now."

Just before Adele left the balcony, Tilda called out to her.

"Adele, did Decklan say what he and Calista had planned? I heard they intended to travel soon."

Adele nodded.

"Yes, they're off to New York for a while, and then possibly Europe."

For a few seconds, Tilda's eyes hardened as her former nature reemerged. She was jealous. That moment soon passed, forcibly pushed away by her improved self. Tilda's head lifted and her shoulders straightened. She gave Adele a reassuring, albeit somewhat forced, smile.

"That's good to hear. They still have a lot of catching up to do. Good day, Ms. Plank. I really do hope to be seeing more of you."

Adele moved down the stairs and exited the hotel on her way to the resort's main parking lot. She paused to look back, expecting to see Tilda watching her from above. The balcony was empty, though. Tilda had retreated into her hotel residence. Adele quickly turned and continued on her way to her car.

Friday Harbor and the Delroy Hicks–created mystery of Avery and Bess Jenkins, and their sudden involvement in Adele's life, beckoned.

3.

"Oh, my goodness! You really did make it to us! Bless old Delroy and his conniving ways!"

Adele found herself being hugged with considerable enthusiasm by seventy-four-year-old Bess Jenkins, who had moved out from behind a small counter near the back of the office space that overlooked the Friday Harbor ferry terminal. Bess was just under five feet tall, very thin, with dark-blue eyes magnified behind a pair of thick-lensed glasses. Her short unkempt gray hair resembled a long-abandoned bird's nest.

"So you really are Adele Plank, huh? The young lady who returned the writer's wife to him!"

Adele stepped back and issued a thin smile.

"Yes, I suppose that's me."

The small, cluttered space that had long served as the office for the *Island Gazette* smelled of saltwater, old paper, and ink. The walls were adorned with framed editions of the publication dating back decades. In the corners were stacks of previous issues precariously piled high atop the heavily scuffed dark-wood floor. Attached to the center of the low cream-colored ceiling buzzed a single florescent light.

An aged male voice erupted from somewhere beyond a back doorway.

"What's the fuss all about, Bess?"

Bess turned her head and yelled back, clearly annoyed by the interruption.

"It's her! Come out and say hello!"

The male voice bellowed a reply.

"Her?"

Bess rolled her eyes.

"The one Delroy told us might one day stop by!"

After a few seconds of silence, the man answered.

"Delroy? Delroy's dead! What the hell are you on about, old woman?"

Bess's face tightened into an exasperated scowl.

"I'm so sorry. I'll be right back."

Adele watched the old woman disappear into the area behind the main office and then heard Bess bickering with someone.

"Now get on out there and stop yelling at me, you lazy old grump!"

The male voice strongly objected to the accusation of being a grump.

"I'm not the one angry here! I was just trying to find out who you were talking to. Why didn't you just say it was the young woman who found Calista Stone? The one Delroy told us about?"

Bess hissed a barrage of mild curse words and then the argument went silent as both Bess and Avery Jenkins emerged from the back room to the front of the office, where Adele stood waiting.

Avery was nearly eighty, just as thin as his wife, with a long, deeply lined face and hands badly bent by the ravages of arthritis. The tips of his fingers were stained by dark ink. His winter-white hair was combed neatly back from a wide and prominent forehead. A tattered brown sweater hung off sloped, bony shoulders and revealed a small hump above his shoulders that was exacerbated by his bent posture. He extended his gnarled right hand and gave Adele a big smile as his deep-set green eyes twinkled with delight.

"Hello, young lady! My name is Avery Jenkins, and this here is my sometimes loving wife, Bess. We've owned and operated the *Island Gazette* for, uh, how long has it been, Bess?"

Adele was careful to shake Avery's arthritic hand gently as Bess rolled her eyes again.

"Forty-nine years, Avery. It'll be fifty in August."

Avery gave Adele a quick wink before replying to his wife.

"August? August Rydel died years ago!"

Bess's mouth opened wide as she prepared to correct her husband once again, but instead she realized what he was up to and shook both her head and finger at him while unable to conceal a smile.

"Oh, you little brat! Having a bit of a laugh, are you?"

Avery placed his hand on the back of Adele's arm and urged her to follow him into the back room.

"This is where the magic happens."

The old man didn't walk so much as shuffle. He looked up and noted Adele watching his slow, deliberate gait.

"As bad as the arthritis has been on my hands, the knees are even worse. Enjoy your youth, young lady. It sure as hell doesn't get any easier."

The back room was nearly the same size as the front space but was dominated by a 1950s printing press. The contraption was an assortment of dark-metal framing and cylinders.

As Adele marveled that something so antiquated could still be used to create a modern newspaper, Avery pointed to the great metallic beast and the rolls of yellowed paper that stood next to it.

"That's what we used when we first started this business. Took hours and hours to get just one page right. Guess that's what some folks would call a work intensive operation."

Bess stepped into the room and waved away her husband's brief history lesson.

"He doesn't use that thing anymore. He's been fooling people with it for twenty years. The entire operation is actually in the corner over there."

Adele looked to where Bess was pointing and found a small desk with an older PC and keyboard connected to a much smaller but similar version of the large antique printing press.

Avery looked disappointed that the ruse was up, but then his face brightened, and he motioned for Adele to follow him to the small work space.

"I can print out the entire newspaper from here, including photos. We can do multiple colors as well, though that means different inks, which cost more, so we try and keep it all black and white except for the front page color photo. What used to take me days years ago can now be done in just a few hours. The world just keeps moving faster and faster, doesn't it?"

Adele found the printing press setup similar, albeit on a smaller scale, to the one she used while working as a member of her college newspaper staff.

Avery folded his arms across his bony chest and then grinned back at Adele.

"So, when do you start?"

Adele's face tightened, indicating her confusion.

"I'm sorry, what?"

"Delroy said you would be looking for a job. Lord knows it's getting too hard for me to check out news stories myself. I can hardly get out of the car, let alone walk any further than across a room. Now I know it's not a big city job by any means, and that most our stories have to do with birthdays, funerals, small business features, and local sports, but from time to time we do have serious news, and it's our job to be the ones to cover it right. Island news should be written up by an islander, so if you plan to stay, you qualify! Your article on Decklan and Calista Stone's twenty-seven-year reunion more than proved your talent, and we'd love to have you on staff."

Adele stood with her mouth half-open as she attempted to digest the details of the surprise job offer. She could almost hear Delroy chuckling as he looked down on her. Bess cleared her throat and peered at Adele with eyes that pleaded for her to accept the position.

"The fact is, Adele, we're getting too old to handle all the requirements of this business. I can manage the books OK, the advertising accounts, but Avery is the writer. He finds the stories, puts them all together, and then goes to print every week. In forty-nine years, he's never missed an issue, *not a single one*. I've tried to help with some of that, but there are days I'm too tired to do much more than try and stay awake, let alone get any work done. We need some help, or I'm afraid this newspaper won't survive the summer. Delroy knew how difficult things were getting for us, and after he met you, it seems he thought it might be something you would be willing to consider."

Avery's face took on the same pleading look as his wife's while he stood waiting for Adele's answer.

"What do you say, Adele? In a few years, the business could be all yours. We'll be here to help with the transition, introduce you to all the local merchants who pay for advertising, and then hand it over when you feel ready."

Adele was about to reply when she heard the entrance door open and then close and a voice call out.

"Hello? Avery, Bess? Are you in here?"

I know that voice.

Adele followed close behind the slow-moving couple and confirmed with her eyes what her ears had already told her. It was Suzanne Blatt, the middle-aged owner of the Friday Harbor bookstore, a woman Adele had first met while doing research for her interview with Decklan. Like before, she was dressed casually in a red T-shirt, tan khakis, and white orthopedic tennis shoes.

Suze immediately recognized Adele.

"Adele! What in the world are you doing here?"

Avery made certain to answer before Adele could.

"She's about ready to join our staff is what she's doing here. Isn't that right, Adele?"

Suze's face broke out into a nearly ear-to-ear smile as she clapped her hands together.

"Oh, that is so wonderful!"

Bess stepped in front of her husband while waving her hands in front of her.

"Wait a minute, wait a gosh-darn minute! This poor young lady hasn't even decided yet. Give her some time to think about it at least, you old coot! Now, Suze, is there something you need?"

Suze's head cocked to the side as she struggled to remember what had her making the crosstown journey to the newspaper office. Then her eyes widened as she snapped her fingers.

"That's right—there's talk of something having been found in the water near Ripple Island. Apparently the new sheriff and the county coroner were out there early this morning shortly after daybreak. An older couple on their boat saw them while heading into Friday Harbor on their way back from Poets Cove in British Columbia. They told me about it not an hour ago at the bookstore. I thought I'd come down here and see if you'd heard anything."

Bess looked at her husband. Avery frowned while shaking his head.

"No, haven't heard a single thing."

The old man's bushy white eyebrows lifted.

"And you know what *that* means, Bess."

Bess nodded.

"It means we have ourselves a story."

Both Avery and Bess turned their heads to look at Adele. It took her a few seconds before she realized what the stares implied. Avery gave Adele a hint of a smile as his eyes once again returned to their former pleading state.

"It appears your coming here on this very day was meant to be, young lady. I can give you your press credentials. I have an old one lying around here somewhere. Head on down to the sheriff's office and ask to speak to Lucas, uh, Sheriff Pine. He's not much older than you. I'm certain you'll get along just fine. He's a local boy, was a heck of a football player. We're all mighty pleased that he's the one who took over the running of the sheriff's office after it was cleaned out following that mess with Calista Stone's imprisonment by the former sheriff. You just ask Lucas for a comment regarding what was found near Ripple Island. See what he says—and get it on the record."

Adele began to chuckle nervously, thinking the request was some kind of joke. A punch line never came, and her chuckle quickly faded.

"Really? Just like that you want me to go talk to the sheriff about something pulled from the water this morning?"

Avery's eyes narrowed. He didn't approve of Adele's dismissive reply.

"Now hold on, Adele. I need you to put your observant glasses on, OK? Think like the investigator I know you are. Suze said there were two people on the scene this morning. Sheriff Pine was one. Now you tell me, who was the other?"

Adele glanced at Suze and then gave her answer.

"The coroner."

Avery nodded like a wise old owl, confident of the lesson he was about to teach Adele.

"And what would be the *only* thing that is likely to get a coroner out of bed at the break of day and travel on a boat out to an abandoned island near the Canadian border?"

"A dead body."

Avery's nodding intensified.

"That's right, a dead body. Most likely scenario would be a drowning victim. Then again, it might be something else, and until we get official word from the sheriff, we have ourselves a mystery in need of solving. Someone died, and it's our job to find out how and, even more importantly, *why*, and deliver that news to the public."

Adele found herself drawn into the job offer like a swimmer being pulled beneath a powerful undertow. Three pairs of eyes stared intently back at her, waiting for her to decide what she intended to do next.

Oh, what the hell.

"OK, I'll do it. I'll go speak with this Sheriff Pine."

The air erupted with the blaring horn of an approaching ferry, signaling the arrival of yet another group of summer visitors to the islands.

And once again, just like that, a new mystery was underway.

4.

"I'm sorry. Sheriff Pine isn't available right now. Would you like to make an appointment?"

The receptionist at the San Juan County Sheriff's Office wore a dark-blue Bellingham University sweatshirt and black jeans. She was a slightly overweight middle-aged woman with short salt-and-pepper hair and a wide, friendly face adorned with black-framed glasses. The plaque on her desk indicated her name was Samantha Boyler. Samantha peered up at Adele from behind her computer monitor while waiting for a response to the offer of making an appointment. Adele reached across the narrow counter that separated the small lobby from the office area.

"Yes, that's fine. Here's my number. Just have him call me when he's available. I'm staying at the marina in Roche Harbor. I can speak with him anytime."

Samantha's already wide smile grew even wider.

"You have a boat there?"

"Yes, it's Delroy's sailboat—Delroy Hicks."

The receptionist's mouth formed a perfect circle as she suddenly realized she knew of Adele.

"Oh, my goodness, you're the college reporter who did the story on the writer and his long-lost wife! I heard you were back on the islands."

Samantha stood up and nervously pulled the bottom of her sweatshirt down over her ample backside as she continued to gush over a local celebrity status that had been to that point, unknown to Adele.

"Your story about that whole terrible mess was just wonderful. Beautifully written, it made me cry and cry and cry. I'll be sure to let the sheriff know you were in. He'll have your number and where you're staying. I'm sure he knows exactly where Delroy kept his boat."

The receptionist glanced at the piece of paper Adele had given her, which indicated her name and number.

"May I ask what this is in regards to, Ms. Plank?"

Adele was about to keep the cause of her visit secret but then decided she wanted to gauge Samantha's reaction to the rumor of a body having been removed from the water that morning.

"I'm looking into reports of a dead body discovered near Ripple Island earlier today."

Samantha's smile dissipated like fog beneath the warm gaze of the sun.

"A body? What body?"

Adele noted that Samantha was either a very good liar, or actually knew nothing of the alleged visit by the sheriff and county coroner to Ripple Island, which in turn would suggest some kind of ongoing cover-up.

"We were given information that a body was pulled from the water early this morning near Ripple Island by the sheriff and the county coroner."

Sensing she was possibly discussing something that might get her into trouble with her new boss, Samantha sat back down in her chair and forced a very brief smile onto her face.

"I'll let the sheriff know you were here, Ms. Plank. He'll be in touch."

Adele gave a quick thank-you and then returned to the world outside the sheriff's red-bricked single-story office building located in the heart of the Friday Harbor business district. The streets were lined with cars; the sidewalks a bustling line of visitors both old and new. Another ferry horn announced the arrival of still more tourists.

White, puffy masses of slow-moving cumulus clouds passed overhead, hinting at a potential evening shower. As Adele stood watching their progress, a new gold SUV with black trim pulled into the parking spot to her left. She watched as a tall, athletically built young man stepped out of the vehicle and gave her a look that was equal parts curiosity and annoyance. His cleanly shaved face was complemented by a dark tan and neatly trimmed brown hair. He removed a pair of gold-framed sunglasses to reveal green-blue eyes that matched the waters surrounding the islands.

"Are you Adele Plank?"

Adele nodded as she realized who was speaking to her.

"Hello, Ms. Plank, I'm Sheriff Lucas Pine. What is it you'd like to talk to me about?"

Sheriff Pine wasn't in uniform. Instead, he had on a pair of worn blue jeans, light-blue tennis shoes, and a simple white T-shirt that did little to hide the outline of the well-formed chest underneath. *Samantha must have called him seconds after I left the office.*

"My receptionist told me you stopped in, and I was just across the street, so here I am. It's my day off, but I'd be happy to sit down and answer any questions you might have. Would you care to come back inside?"

Adele found the young sheriff's voice to be pleasant. Not overly deep, both friendly and confident, and with a hint of a Southern drawl unusual for someone Adele thought to have been born and raised in the Pacific Northwest.

"That would be fine, Sheriff, thank you."

Adele could feel Samantha's eyes staring at her as she passed by the reception counter and into the short hallway that led to the back of the office building. Sheriff Pine opened a door on his right at the end of the hallway and then motioned for Adele to follow him inside. His office was a twelve-by-twelve space with a single small window overlooking a cluster of flowered shrubs. The walls were covered in framed photographs of the sheriff as a high school and college football player. The largest of these pictures showed him wearing a military uniform and indicated his graduation from Army Basic Combat Training in Fort Sill, Oklahoma. A date on the bottom stated it had been taken just over three years ago.

"You were in the military?"

Sheriff Pine sat down behind a metal-framed desk and motioned for Adele to take a seat in one of two chairs that were placed against the wall nearest the door.

"Yes, I was. Did three years after I graduated college with a degree in criminal justice."

"And where did you go to college?"

The sheriff pointed to a picture of a football team that hung on the wall to his left.

"University of North Alabama. It's a Division II school, not the big-time like folks around here like to tell it. I was the backup quarterback there for four years. Never started a game—not even my senior year. They paid for my degree, though, and the army did the same with my law enforcement training, and now here I am, the youngest county sheriff in the state. I guess that counts for something."

"That must be where you picked up that bit of Southern accent."

Sheriff Pine leaned back in his chair with his arms folded across his chest and grinned.

"You're not the first to say that, but I never noticed. I figure I'm talking the way I always have, but who knows? A man spends six or so years somewhere else, I suppose he starts to sound like that other place."

An uncomfortable pause inserted itself into the middle of their initial small talk. The sheriff leaned forward and narrowed his eyes just enough to let Adele know he intended to find out exactly what her motivations were regarding stories of dead bodies being plucked from the water.

"Ms. Plank, as you are likely already aware, I'm new to this job. As such, I have a lot of eyes and ears keeping tabs on how I do in the coming months. I also realize my sitting at this desk is due in no small part to your own involvement in Mr. and Mrs. Stone's reunion. Though he was long retired, what you uncovered regarding former Sheriff Speaks has placed this department under intense scrutiny from the state authorities—and for good reason. It was a mess. The people of this county have put their trust in me to try and clean it up, and that's what I intend to do. So, with that said, how about you explain to me why you are telling my receptionist about a dead body having been found near Ripple Island?"

Adele wasn't about to allow herself to be intimidated or charmed by the handsome young sheriff. She met his stare with one of her own.

"Because she asked me why I was here, and I told her. My question to *you*, Sheriff, is why your receptionist doesn't know of it already?"

Sheriff Pine's mouth tightened as he cleared his throat.

"What exactly do you think you know about what may or may not have been found near Ripple Island, Ms. Plank?"

Adele smiled as her confidence grew. She was enjoying this bit of cat and mouse with the new sheriff.

"You were out there early this morning with the coroner. That means it involved a human body. I'm simply trying to find out if it was an accidental drowning or something else."

The sheriff shifted in his seat.

He's nervous.

"Why do want to know this? Are you still writing for your college newspaper?"

Adele shook her head and removed the press pass from her back pocket that Avery had given her just an hour earlier. She put the pass on top of the desk and slid it toward the sheriff.

"I've taken a position with the *Island Gazette*."

Sheriff Pine grunted.

"You're working for Avery and Bess?"

"That's right."

The sheriff lightly rapped the top of his desk with the knuckles of both his hands as he considered this new bit of information.

"I tell you what, Ms. Plank. I have nothing I can report to you officially at this point, but when I do, I'll be sure to let you know."

Adele wasn't yet ready to give up.

"How about you confirm or deny that a body was in fact found in the water this morning near Ripple Island?"

Sheriff Pine stood up from behind his desk and motioned with his left hand toward the door.

"I'm afraid we're done for now, Ms. Plank. As I just said, I don't have anything to give you on the record at this time."

Adele was about to turn toward the door but then paused.

"What about off the record?"

The sheriff's jaw clenched. For a moment, he appeared ready for an angry outburst, but instead his eyes softened, and he chuckled.

"I don't know you well enough to give you that courtesy, Ms. Plank. Perhaps someday."

The sheriff gently escorted Adele out of the building. He stood just inside the glass entrance door and watched her as she made her way back to her parked car on the other side of the street.

Don't let him know which car you drive.

Adele walked past her MINI and continued down the sidewalk until she rounded a corner and was out of sight of the sheriff's office. She stood there for several minutes until she spotted the sheriff's SUV drive slowly by on its way toward the ferry terminal. Only then did she return to her car, get inside, and drive herself back to Roche Harbor, periodically glancing in the rearview mirror to make certain she wasn't being followed. Though Sheriff Lucas Pine appeared to be a man both earnest and likable, Adele remained unconvinced he was worthy of her trust, and she intended to keep it that way until he proved otherwise.

A few hours later found her waking up after a short nap inside Delroy's sailboat. She still found it difficult to consider it *her* boat. Perhaps in time, but not just yet. Adele hadn't intended to fall asleep, but the warm weather combined with the constant soft slap of small waves against the boat's hull made it nearly impossible to stay awake as she lay out on the small bed encased within the sailboat's bow.

The quiet, comfortable solitude inside of Adele's new home was shattered by the sound of her cell phone, which she had left on the counter near the sink. With a soft groan, she pushed herself out of the bed and answered the call.

"Hello?"

Without a response from the other end, the call was ended. Adele looked down to see her phone indicated the number was restricted.

She opened the sailboat's door and stepped outside and then onto the dock. The temperature had dropped considerably due to the clouds that had been pushed in by a quickening breeze. Despite the change in weather, Roche Harbor remained cheerfully busy with visitors. Adele looked to her left and to her right and then scanned the multiple buildings clustered along the shoreline.

I'm being watched.

Though she was without proof, Adele's instincts convinced her it was so. She looked up toward Tilda's balcony, where the hotel owner was so often seen observing the comings and goings of Roche Harbor below, but found the balcony empty. Adele was startled as her phone began ringing in her hand. She looked down to see it was Avery Jenkins.

"Hello, Mr. Jenkins."

"No need to be calling me Mr. Jenkins, young lady. Avery's fine. Were you able to speak with the sheriff?"

Adele made certain to keep her voice low enough so that the conversation couldn't be overhead by anyone who might be standing nearby.

"Yes. He basically gave me a no comment."

Though she couldn't see him, Adele knew Avery was smiling.

"Is that so? Well then, what do you suggest, Adele? Think of it as *your* newspaper. How would you get the sheriff to open up?"

Now it was Adele who was smiling.

"I'd run a front page article on the rumor of a body being found near Ripple Island and note how the sheriff's office had no comment. To the reader, that no comment would indicate the rumor is true. The community will then demand the sheriff give them an answer, and he'll be forced to do just that if he has any hope of controlling the story."

"Very good, Adele, that's *exactly* how we're going to do it. Now, once the new issue is distributed, there will likely be a bit of backlash. One can't rock the boat without first making a few waves. Sheriff Pine probably won't care for you much for a while, but I'm willing to wager he'll sure as hell respect you more and won't be so quick to give you a *no comment* in the future."

Adele once again felt the presence of unseen eyes upon her. As she held the phone to her ear, she looked around trying to locate the source.

"We'll see about that, Avery. I'll be by early tomorrow. See you then."

The call ended just as the first droplets of early evening rain began to fall and a gust of wind pushed against Adele's face. Still certain she was being spied upon, Adele retreated to the sailboat, closed the door behind her, and locked it.

She was no longer tired.

Outside, both rain and darkness increased, while a pair of midnight eyes looked out from the gathering gloom and continued to stare at Adele's new home.

5.

"I'm happy to see you chose to stay here for a while, young lady. It's a good fit, you and these islands."

In her dream, Delroy Hicks was just as Adele remembered him. The low voice juxtaposed within the emaciated, deeply lined, hard-edged face, and an especially thin body that was seemingly all elbows and knees.

The ever-present fedora was perched atop the former college professor's white-haired head, and so, too, were the deeply scuffed leather sandals attached to his well-traveled feet.

"You're dead, so I must be dreaming."

Delroy's light-blue eyes gave off an amused gleam when he smiled.

"Bah! What do we primates know of death? It's mere arrogance to assume much of anything regarding that subject. All you need concern yourself with, my dear Adele, is the here and the now. Live this life, and live it well."

Adele shook her head.

"I don't know how to do that. I feel lost."

Delroy folded his right knee over his left and rested his hands on top of them.

"One cannot be found until one is first lost, yeah? Don't concern yourself with having to be somewhere you think you are required to be. Rather, hope to find yourself where you were *meant* to be. That's where you'll be most content because that's where you'll find yourself."

Delroy's voice was so clear, so *real*, Adele began to wonder if he was somehow actually there sitting in front of her.

"Maybe I don't want to find myself. Maybe I won't like who I find."

Delroy gave Adele a dismissive wave from a bony-fingered hand.

"Nonsense! You're just feeling a bit misplaced, is all. That's perfectly normal at this point in your life. You've spent years in college. That gave you a sense of purpose, of one year building onto the next. Now, you don't have that. You have to create your own sense of purpose, and it's not so clearly outlined as before. I'll tell you this, though: success in life is far more important, more lasting, yet more difficult to attain, than any kind of success in the academic world."

"I'm afraid I'm going to fail."

Delroy closed his eyes and sat silently for several seconds before continuing.

"Success, *real* success, doesn't come without failure. Most often, one precedes the other. The trick is to learn from that failure. Some do, many don't. I have every reason to believe you're the learning kind. I know people, and even though our time working together was brief, I know *you*, Adele Plank."

The corners of Adele's mouth collapsed into a troubled frown.

"That makes one of us."

Adele's dream version of Delroy suddenly changed the subject.

"Tell me about this new mystery."

"There's not much to tell. Rumors of a body found in the water near a little island by the Canadian border. The new sheriff doesn't seem too keen on talking about it with me."

Delroy leaned forward and flashed an impish grin.

"So, what do you think of our new young sheriff?"

Adele had no interest in taking the bait. Instead, she merely shrugged to show her disinterest, though she admitted to herself that she was looking forward to seeing Sheriff Pine again.

"He's OK. Seems a bit unsure of himself."

"I've always found some humility makes a man that much more attractive."

Again, Adele refused to play along with dream-Delroy's matchmaking intentions.

"I don't have time for a relationship right now. Plus, he's hiding something, and unless I find out what, I can't trust him."

Delroy leaned back until his face nearly disappeared entirely into the darkness of the sailboat's interior.

"Be very careful using time as an excuse, Adele. I watched people tell themselves that very thing year after year after year, until finally there was no next time left to them, and all that remained was regret for all the things not done. Regret is quite possibly the worst ending to a life one can have."

Adele was about to respond when she both heard and felt a heavy thump from somewhere outside the boat. When she looked over at the space Delroy had just occupied, she found it empty. He was gone.

The sound repeated itself again and again, growing louder each time.

Adele opened her eyes and was startled to find bright daylight shining through the small circular window housed just above the sink.

What time is it?

She stood up from the couch, peered through the window, and saw a pair of large black boots moving about on the dock. After unleashing an especially long yawn and then wiping the sleep from her eyes, Adele opened the door and stepped outside, where she saw the full-bearded face of Old Jack staring back at her.

"Uh, hello there, Ms. Plank. I wasn't aware you were inside. I apologize if I woke you. Mr. Stone instructed me to deliver his runabout to your slip here. He was hoping you could keep an eye on it for him while he and Mrs. Stone are away. He says you're free to use it all you like. I've checked it over myself. She's running perfect—a real beauty."

Old Jack looked almost exactly the same as when Adele last saw him over a year ago, after the longtime marine mechanic helped Delroy save Decklan Stone from drowning himself in the waters of Deer Harbor in nearby Orcas Island. His beard was as full and unruly as before. His shiny scalp had perhaps even less hair, and the large, expressive brown eyes were just as kind and shy as she remembered them. His smell was the same, too: gasoline, oil, and seawater.

"I tied her up right alongside your sailboat with a few bumpers hanging off the side to prevent one hull from damaging the other when the weather picks up. I left my business card under the dash. You have any mechanical trouble, just give me a ring, and I'll be out this way to take a look."

"How are you getting back home?"

Jack motioned behind him with his thumb.

"Got another customer's boat here I'm picking up and driving back to my shop in Orcas. Just swapping one out for the other."

Adele stepped onto the dock with a friendly, albeit somewhat sleepy smile.

"Thank you so much. Be careful going back."

Jack gave a quick nod, took two long strides away from Adele's sailboat, and then turned around.

"Just wanted you to know it's nice to see you back on the islands, Ms. Plank. You're what my father would call good people, and we can always use more of those around here."

Adele was surprised and grateful for the compliment.

"Thank you so much, Jack. I'm glad to be back. It really is a beautiful place."

Old Jack's head lifted upward as he took in the cloudless, late-morning blue sky.

"Yes, yes it is. Looks like the last of the bad weather has moved on. Don't think we'll be getting any more rain for at least a week. Good day to you, Ms. Plank."

Adele watched the mechanic move off toward another part of the marina. She turned around to look at the classic 1960s runabout that had been used to transport Delroy and herself on a terrifying night journey upon angry waters from Roche Harbor to Decklan Stone's home some six nautical miles away in Deer Harbor. At the time, Adele thought it might very well be the last journey she would ever take. Delroy proved a more than capable captain, though, and managed to move the small watercraft through worsening wind and waves and eventually to the safety of Decklan's island home.

"She's a beauty."

Adele whirled around to find an older man of average height and build standing just a few feet behind her. His long brown-and-silver hair was tied in a ponytail that hung well below his shoulders. He wore a tattered light-brown Windbreaker, tan cargo shorts, and a pair of old white-and-red Nike Jordan basketball shoes that looked to have almost none of the rubber soles remaining. The face was nearly entirely hidden behind a heavy brown-and-gray beard, and above that beard Adele found herself looking into a pair of the darkest eyes she had ever seen.

"Thanks, but it's not mine. I'm just watching it for a friend."

"Hmmm, you must be an especially capable individual to have someone entrust you with the care of such a beautiful example of a bygone era of American marine craftsmanship."

Adele's internal alarms sounded. It wasn't so much that she felt the man to be a threat; it was just that he seemed rather odd yet strangely familiar to her, even though his bedraggled appearance gave him the look of a homeless person.

"Do I know you?"

The man's gaze dropped to his feet.

"No, I'm certain you don't. Not *personally*, anyways."

Adele sensed him preparing to leave and quickly posed another question, wanting to keep him there for a little longer so she could determine who he was.

"Are you staying at the marina?"

"I have a boat here, but I'm actually staying with an old friend. Perhaps we'll see each other again soon. Until then, I'll let you get back to whatever it was you were doing."

The stranger turned and walked quickly toward the marina entrance. Adele waited to see if he would turn around to look back at her. He didn't. Instead, he disappeared into the gathering throng of tourists who were descending upon another Roche Harbor summer day.

Well, that was interesting.

Adele heard her cell phone ringing and went inside the sailboat to answer it.

"Adele, this is Avery. Just a quick heads up. The new issue of the paper started to be delivered not more than an hour ago, and I've had a visit from the sheriff already. I think he might be on his way to see you. As expected, he's none too happy with our "no comment" story regarding rumors of that body being found out by Ripple Island."

As soon as Avery spoke those words, Adele saw the tall, well-built form of Sheriff Pine striding quickly down the dock toward her slip. He wore the olive-colored shirt and black slacks of his sheriff's uniform, which lent him an air of determined authority she had not noted on him the prior day.

And he looks pretty pissed.

Adele stepped back outside and waited for the sheriff. She didn't have to wait long.

He stopped, took a deep breath, and then quickly ran a hand over his short brown hair as he struggled to keep his tone professional.

"I understand you are doing a job, Ms. Plank. I only ask that you understand that I'm trying to do *my* job, too. You've stirred up a real hornet's nest for me. I've taken calls from every member of the county council asking what the hell is going on, and it's all because of that news article. By the end of the day, everyone on these islands is going to be accusing me of some damn cover-up!"

Adele felt bad for the newly appointed sheriff, but she also knew he was partly responsible for his own predicament.

"*Is* it a cover-up, Sheriff Pine? I asked if there was a body found in the waters near Ripple Island. You refused to give me an answer. The newspaper simply relayed that non-answer to the public, a public that *does* have a right to know."

Sheriff Pine exhaled loudly through his nose. He looked around to see if anyone else was trying to listen in on the conversation.

"I tell you what, Ms. Plank. How about you and I have a sit-down tonight? Call it an interview if you want. Whatever, I don't really care. I'll answer your questions as best I can. All I ask is that the next time you intend to drop a bomb on my head, you at least give me the courtesy of knowing first, OK?"

Adele was quick to agree.

"That's more than fair, Sheriff. What time tonight?"

"My shift is over at six. I have a place on Spring Lane about three miles outside Friday Harbor. I'll text you the address later. I cook a decent burger. We can have a bite and then do the interview."

"We can't meet somewhere in town? Or here on my boat?"

The sheriff shook his head.

"My place is private. I don't need people seeing you and me together. That wouldn't be good for either of us right now."

Adele thought over the risk of being a guest at the home of a man she hardly knew, pushed away her concern, and nodded.

"All right, I'll be there. I'll wait for your text. Just remember—you promised to answer my questions."

Sheriff Pine's smile was strained, like a rubber band being pulled too tight, but Adele appreciated the effort.

"I'll do my best, Ms. Plank."

The sheriff left Adele standing alone on the dock. She took a deep breath, enjoying the clean salt-tinged air as the brisk morning temperatures were giving way to the arriving afternoon warmth. The boat traffic into and out of the resort's marina was increasing. Adele marveled at the variety of watercraft, from yachts in excess of sixty feet to small runabouts like the one that was now tied up next to her sailboat and all manner and sizes of vessels in between. That's when she realized she hadn't yet actually driven a boat herself. She intended to learn, and wondered if her evening meeting with the sheriff went well, that he might someday join her on the water.

Adele's phone indicated it was nearly 11:00 a.m. Her day was off to an unusually late start. After ducking back into the sailboat to freshen up and put on a clean pair of khakis and a tan T-shirt, she began to make her way down the main dock toward the marina entrance and the large paved lot to the west, where her car was parked. Before turning toward the parking lot, she stopped, once again feeling as if someone were staring at her. People moved around her on all sides, making it difficult for Adele to see much farther than a few feet beyond where she stood.

Her eyes shifted upward, scanning the Roche Harbor Hotel. There she saw movement behind a second-floor lace-curtained window, a brief glimpse of a bearded face and a pair of especially dark eyes. It appeared Adele's instincts were correct.

She was being watched.

6.

Adele parked her car on the street directly behind Sheriff Pine's SUV. She was mildly surprised to find the sheriff's residence to be a beautifully crafted two-story white Victorian home with yellow trim. It was partially hidden behind a row of tall pine trees. The yard was meticulously maintained, highlighted by a thick garden of red roses that grew on either side of the covered porch. The house stood back from the street some fifty yards, its entrance marked by a stone path leading to the front door.

Just before she pressed the doorbell, the front door was pulled open, and a tall, elderly man dressed in a tan button-down sweater-vest and black slacks looked at her with a wide, friendly smile affixed to his time-worn face. Though older, the years had not fully diminished his handsome features. A full head of silver hair was combed neatly back from his forehead, which further emphasized a strong square jaw and prominent cheekbones.

"Hello, did you have an appointment?"

Sheriff Pine, wearing a gray sweatshirt and jeans, emerged behind the old man and gently pulled him back from the door before motioning for Adele to step inside.

"Sorry about that, my dad gets confused these days. When he heard you walking up the steps, he thought you were my mother. Normally, he'd be taking a nap about now, but for some reason he seems a little agitated today."

The sheriff turned to face his father, who was still staring at Adele.

"Dad, this is my friend Adele Plank. She's just visiting."

The old man glanced at Adele and then looked back at his son. For several seconds his lips pursed together tightly as he struggled to comprehend what had just been told to him. Then he straightened up, making himself almost as tall as the sheriff, and gave Adele a welcoming nod. She noticed how his blue eyes were suddenly more focused, indicating a comprehension that wasn't there just seconds before.

"Hello, Ms. Plank. I'm Dr. Edmund Pine, Lucas's father. Welcome to our home."

Adele shook the older man's hand.

"Thank you. It's beautiful."

Edmund appeared pleased by the compliment. He smiled and then motioned for Adele to join him in the sitting room, which was just to the left of the foyer entrance. The home smelled of freshly cut roses and the oil used to keep the aged wood floors gleaming. The walls were adorned with neatly placed framed pictures dating back several decades. One of those pictures was of a much younger Edmund Pine standing on his front lawn holding Lucas when the sheriff was just a toddler. Next to them was a beautiful dark-haired woman wearing a black dress. She was grinning for the camera as she rested her head on the doctor's shoulder. Adele pointed to the photograph.

"Is that your mom?"

Lucas nodded.

"Yeah, she passed away a few years ago. It was a stroke."

The sheriff was unable to fully hide the residual pain that still remained from the loss of his mother.

"Her name was Katarina, but everyone just called her Kat. Her family came from Russia. They were Jewish and escaped before the communists took over. It's been tough for us not having her here. More than anyone, she made this house a home."

Within just a few minutes of her arrival, Adele had witnessed an entirely different side to Sheriff Pine—and she liked what she saw. He was more reflective, almost vulnerable, without giving up any of his exterior masculinity. Dr. Pine's voice called out from the sitting room.

"Rest here next to me, uh, young lady, and tell me what brings you by."

Adele sat down next to Edmund on a cream-colored, early twentieth-century antique couch that faced a small, red-bricked fireplace over which hung a large and beautiful oil-painting of Friday Harbor that depicted the hillside city's lights gleaming off early evening waters.

"Ah, you notice that painting there, do you? My wife did it. She's the most beautiful and talented little thing! Speaking of which, Lucas, do you know where Kat is? Is she upstairs?"

Adele felt her heart nearly break as Dr. Pine stood up and walked out of the room, where he then stopped at the bottom of the stairs.

"Kat, honey, come on down and meet Lucas's new girlfriend!"

Whatever discomfort Adele felt was reflected in the sheriff's eyes tenfold. No matter how often he had to watch his father suffer his episodes of dementia, it was never easier, especially as they gradually became worse.

"Dad, she's not here. Remember, Mom passed away."

Edmund whirled around to face his son, anger flashing in his eyes.

"Don't be ridiculous, Lucas! Who's been taking care of your mother's roses if not her? Of course she's here. Shame on you for saying otherwise! It's not funny. Sometimes, your sense of humor is nothing more than badly disguised cruelty!"

"Dad, maybe it's time you had a nap. You look tired. Let me take you upstairs."

The elder Pine's fatigued eyes glowered as he looked from Adele to his son.

"You know the rules, Lucas. You think I'm so gullible as to leave you down here alone with one of your lady friends? Your mother made it quite clear to you. We're not one of those *evolved* parents who let their kids run around at all hours unattended. I've seen the results of that far too many times in my practice. Young girls pregnant, and young boys all too willing to simply move on to the next conquest. Shameful! And I blame the parents as much as I do those poor, stupid children!"

Lucas shook his head.

"It's not like that, Dad. She's a guest, not a little girl. I'm not in school anymore, remember? I'm the San Juan County sheriff. I leave the house every morning wearing a uniform."

Adele could sense the worsening confusion building up within the retired doctor's voice, a confusion that quickly bordered on outright panic.

"Uniform? But you've been out of the army for . . . it's been years now, right? You were almost out by the time your mother . . ."

Edmund's voice trailed off as his eyes scanned the interior of a home he had lived in for decades but more recently had moments where he hardly recognized it. His shoulders slumped and his eyes closed. He had just enough of the experienced physician residing somewhere within his distracted globe to realize there was something very wrong. That he was no longer himself and most likely would never be again.

"I'm tired, son. I'd like to lie down."

Lucas whispered to Adele.

"I'll be right back, and then I can make us something to eat."

"I'm fine. Take as much time as you need."

Adele listened as father and son made their way upstairs. She could hear the soft shuffle of footsteps, bits of conversation, and then a door being closed.

The sheriff returned downstairs and motioned for Adele to follow him into a small lavender-colored kitchen at the back of the house.

Lucas pulled out a chair from a white table that sat next to a tall window that overlooked the fenced back garden. Early-evening shadows extended over the dark green grass and the wood deck that was just beyond a narrow door leading from the kitchen to the yard. The kitchen was a square twenty-by-twenty space, illuminated by a single silver light fixture in the center of the room's low ceiling. The floors were white and black checkers, a design Adele knew to have been popular in the 1950's.

"He's already asleep. I knew he was tired. Can I get you something to drink? Water, tea, some coffee?"

Adele shook her head. She wanted to make it clear to the sheriff she was there on business.

"I'm fine, thanks."

Sheriff Pine held up a black cast-iron skillet.

"This is the same pan my mom used for as long as I can remember. I'm gonna make us a couple of white-bread burgers. You don't have to eat yours, but maybe by the time they are done you'll want to join me."

Adele gave a short nod, worrying that the time spent at the sheriff's house wouldn't give her the information he had promised to share with her.

"You mind if I ask you some questions while you cook?"

The sheriff paused while holding a loaf of bread in one hand and a pound of paper-wrapped ground beef in the other.

"Yeah, go ahead. I said I'd answer your questions as best I could, right?"

Adele folded her hands on the table and smiled.

"That's right."

Lucas turned toward the white electric stove, turned up the heat under the pan, and began to form two hamburger patties.

"So go ahead, Ms. Plank, fire away."

Adele had to raise her voice so she could be heard over the sound of hissing meat as it struck the hot skillet.

"The body you found, do you know who it is?"

The sheriff shook his head while watching the sizzling burger patties.

"No. All we have are the bones the coroner sent off to Seattle for forensics. There are currently multiple missing female cases in Washington State and British Columbia alone, so at this point, we have no idea who she might be."

Adele silently noted the victim was female, while she also seized upon what she knew to be another critical piece of information.

"You said you found bones. It wasn't actually a complete body?"

Lucas appeared not to have heard Adele's question. He flipped the patties over, waited, and then placed one of the patties on top of a slice of bread, added a large portion of ketchup, several shakes of salt and pepper, and then another slice of bread over the top. He handed Adele her plate and sat down across the table from her with his own plated burger in front of him.

"Did you hear me?"

The sheriff nodded as he took a bite of his burger.

"Yeah, I heard you. I figure it's a good idea we finish eating before discussing what was or wasn't left of the body when we found it. You want a beer?"

Initially, Adele was going to refuse the offer but then realized a beer sounded good.

"Sure."

Lucas quickly moved to the fridge and withdrew two bottles of a local microbrew labeled Island-Time Ale. He opened both bottles and handed one to Adele.

Over the course of the following thirty minutes, the sheriff and Adele spoke about seemingly everything but the case of the body with no name. He shared stories of his days as the local high school football star, how that stardom meant little once he reached college, and then his realization a life in the military wasn't for him, either.

"I knew I wanted to come back home. My mom was gone, my dad needed help, and once the sheriff's position was offered to me, it was a done deal. So, here I am, small-town boy becomes a small-time sheriff."

Adele in turn explained her uncertainty after graduation, how the short-term fame that followed her article on Decklan and Calista Stone's remarkable reunion made her rethink her values, which up to that point she wasn't entirely sure she even possessed. At the end of those thirty minutes, they had eaten both burgers and were sipping from their second beer.

"It must be tough seeing your father struggle like that."

Lucas's wide shoulders lifted slightly and then dropped.

"He probably delivered half the people living on these islands. He loved his work, loved helping people. My parents were older when they had me. They had tried to have kids for years, gave up, and then just like that, my mom was pregnant. She was almost fifty by the time I was born. She called me her miracle boy."

A brief moment of silence ensued, but it felt much longer. Adele knew it was time to ask questions regarding the ongoing investigation, just as the sheriff knew he had to deliver on his promise to answer them.

Lucas opened a third beer, took a long drink, and then proceeded to share the grim details of what he had earlier pulled from the waters near Ripple Island.

"It was a crab pot. The body had been broken up into pieces and stuffed into the pot, and the crabs, well, they did what crabs do. They picked it clean."

Adele's beer was halfway to her mouth. She abruptly put it down.

"Oh my god."

The sheriff nearly emptied his beer and then wiped his mouth with the back of his hand. He remained as horrified by what he had found as Adele was upon first hearing of it.

"Yeah, it was, uh, pretty shocking."

Adele realized the information had taken another critical turn.

"It's a murder case."

Lucas nodded slowly.

"It would appear so. I don't know of anyone who stuffs themselves into a crab pot and then manages to toss it overboard. That's why I was trying to keep this contained for now. The county council, they're so damn nervous over any kind of negative news at the height of the tourist season. There was your story from last year, that terrible thing that was done to Calista Stone, and now this? It has all the makings of a public relations disaster. I wasn't even born yet the last time we had an open murder investigation around these islands."

Soon, the sheriff was well into his fourth beer, and Adele was approaching comfortably numb status after nearly completing her third. He again promised to give her the first copy of the official statement from the sheriff's office regarding the recently discovered body so she could publish it in the newspaper. Adele in turn promised not to be so quick to paint him into the proverbial corner regarding information pertaining to a sensitive and ongoing investigation. It was a sincerely given and much-appreciated truce between the two of them.

And then Lucas did something unexpected. He asked Adele for help.

"How you saved Calista Stone, how you put the pieces of that puzzle together so quickly, I could use that kind of talent, Ms. Plank. If you see or hear anything regarding this case, please let me know."

"You mean we'd sort of be like two young island-hopping crime-fighting partners?"

The sheriff grinned as he lifted his bottle and lightly tapped it against Adele's.

"Sure. Here's to new partners."

While a new partnership was being forged inside the Pine residence, someone stood outside hidden in darkness, watching with rage-filled eyes from across the street.

And waiting.

7.

Adele woke to the comforting scent of freshly brewed coffee. Sheriff Pine emerged from the kitchen with a cup in hand and offered it to her.

"If you're anything like me, morning without coffee is unthinkable."

She sat up in the pullout couch that had been her bed following the late-night conversation that was accompanied by far more beer than she was accustomed to drinking. The sheriff looked no worse for wear. In fact, Adele found that he cut a rather dashing figure in his fitted sheriff's uniform. She reached out to accept the coffee, cradling the warm cup in both her hands.

"Thank you. What time is it?"

Lucas glanced down at his watch as he eased himself into a cushioned chair opposite the couch.

"Just after seven."

The sound of a shower running upstairs filtered down to the living room.

"That's Dad. He's best in the morning—almost normal. Then he gets tired and more confused as the day goes on. I have a retired nurse come by before I head off to work. Her name is Maxine. She was on staff with Dad at the clinic for years before his condition required he retire. She stays here with him most the day. Takes him for a walk, tends to the roses. The roses are important. Mom kept the house filled with fresh-cut flowers, so Maxine makes sure to do the same. It makes Dad feel like a part of Mom is still around, which seems to calm him."

While Lucas spoke, Adele's eyes scanned the collection of framed photographs that hung on the walls and the athletic trophies placed on the fireplace mantel. Most of the pictures were of Lucas at various ages, and many of those showed him wearing a football jersey. When the sheriff noticed Adele staring at the photos, his face tightened into a grimace.

"If I had my way, I'd take those things down, but Dad likes them there."

"You were quite the stud, Sheriff Pine."

Lucas issued a soft grunt and shook his head.

"Uh, yeah, like I said, my dad demands the pictures stay put. Mom put them all up."

Both the sheriff and Adele turned at the sound of footsteps coming down the stairs. Dr. Pine entered the room wearing dark slacks and a crisp, open-collared white dress shirt with the sleeves rolled up. He gave Adele a wide smile.

"Good morning! I hope that old couch wasn't too uncomfortable."

Adele returned the doctor's smile with an equally warm one of her own.

"Not at all."

Edmund turned toward his son.

"Lucas, did you offer your guest some breakfast?"

Before the sheriff could respond, Adele interjected.

"I'm fine, really. I have to be going soon. I plan on checking in with Avery and Bess and then speaking with Suze after that."

The doctor's brow furrowed as he struggled to recall the names being told to him. Lucas was quick to help his father remember.

"Suze, she owns the bookstore."

Doctor Pine's eyes widened as he snapped his fingers.

"Yes, of course! Well please tell Suze hello for me, Adele. Now, if you don't mind, I'm off to make my oatmeal."

Lucas watched his dad disappear into the kitchen. Adele noticed the sheriff's eyes had narrowed just a bit, as if he were uncertain of something.

"What is it?"

The sheriff peered over the brim of his coffee cup as he took a long sip.

"He remembered your name. That's unusual. You must have made an impression."

Adele shrugged.

"Well, I *am* rather remarkable, so that doesn't really surprise me."

Lucas's head fell back as he filled the living room with laughter.

Adele found she liked the sound—a lot. A short time later she was heading out the Pine family's front door with both the sheriff and his father watching her walk back to her car. She paused to give both men a quick wave and then started the MINI and made her way to the newspaper office, where she knew Bess and Avery were waiting.

Friday Harbor was also in the process of awakening. Brightly colored storefronts hinted at the bustle of summer business to come, while numerous residents dotted the sidewalks, walking dogs, jogging, or taking care of various other tasks before the streets became too congested with tourists. Even the loud cries of the seagulls as they flew overhead seemed to indicate their determination to finish up their morning duties before the place was overrun with people.

Bess, wearing a dark sweater and jeans, answered Adele's knock on the newspaper office's door. With a quick smile, the older woman motioned for Adele to come in.

"No need to knock, Adele. This is where you work."

Avery emerged from the back office. He wore a pair of loose-fitting tan cargo shorts with black socks pulled up nearly to his knees, and a denim jacket. He was moving slowly and appeared to be limping.

"Woke up to my knees yelling at me again. Some mornings are like that, but enough of my complaining. Did you speak with the sheriff more about that body pulled from the water?"

Adele nodded.

"He gave me the details, at least some of them."

Avery looked at Adele with widened eyes as Bess, who stood directly behind her husband, did the same.

"And?"

"It's a murder case, a rather gruesome one."

Avery grunted.

"I knew it!"

He turned toward Bess, his voice a low, serious-toned whisper.

"Order up the scones, Bess. This requires a staff meeting. Jose should be here soon."

While Bess disappeared into the back office area, Avery turned to Adele.

"Jose is our delivery guy. He distributes each issue around San Juan, Orcas, Shaw, and Lopez islands. Been with us for almost ten years. He's a real nice fella, and I know he'll like you."

As if on cue, the front door opened and a short, heavily built Hispanic man in his mid-thirties walked in. He had a wide, clean-shaved, friendly face, complemented by medium-length dark hair that constantly threatened to fall over his eyes and barely covered a pair of abnormally large ears.

"There you are, Jose. I'd like you to meet Adele Plank. She's going to be taking over some of the writing duties for us."

Jose straightened his posture and tugged on his red T-shirt in an effort to hide the potbelly he had developed in recent years due to his love of all things chocolate and beer.

"Hello, Ms. Plank."

Adele smiled, trying to set the clearly shy Jose at ease. She was also charmed by the hint of an accent he seemed so determined to hide.

"Nice to meet you, Jose."

Jose returned the smile and then looked up to see an excited Bess returning to the front office.

"I thought I heard you come in, Jose. Did you get everything delivered?"

Jose nodded.

"Yes, just got back from Shaw."

Again the front door opened and a wide-hipped middle-aged woman wearing an oversize, flower-patterned dress, walked through. Her blonde-gray hair was pulled back in a ponytail.

"Got your scones, Bess! Be careful, though, they're still hot!"

The office filled with the warm scent of fresh-made pastry. As Bess took the white bag, Avery pointed to Adele.

"Beatrice, I'd like you to meet Adele Plank. Adele, this is Beatrice Baker. She owns Beatrice Breads on the second floor. She's been renting from us for, my goodness almost twenty years. It's no lie when I tell you, this woman cooks the best pastries in the islands. And these scones, well, you are truly in for a treat!"

Beatrice gave Adele a firm handshake and addressed her in a loud, confident voice.

"Hi there, Adele! Enjoy those scones and be sure to come back for more! Now, I got to get going. There will be a couple hundred passengers coming off the next ferry, and I only have half the inventory I'll need ready by the time they get here."

Avery was already making his way to the back room and the fresh-baked pastry. He rubbed his hands together as he did so, clearly looking forward to the impromptu snack.

Soon Adele sat down at a small, round, plastic table opposite Avery, with Bess to Adele's left, and Jose to her right. Each had a paper plate with a scone and napkin in front of them. Avery's scone was already half-eaten by the time Bess convened the staff meeting.

"OK, let's get started. It seems clear the paper is sitting on a big story, and this next issue is going to be the first real telling of this information to the community. Jose, we're going to add another thousand copies for this next issue, so be prepared for a bit more delivery work. Give yourself some extra time."

Jose nodded as he started to swallow a mouthful of scone.

Avery finished the last of his pastry and then cleared his throat.

"Adele, I assume you plan on attending tonight's council meeting. A few folks might show up to ask questions about the body that was found. You'll want to be there to take notes detailing how members of the council respond. There might also be a formal statement on the matter from the sheriff."

Adele looked up from her scone, caught unaware by the mention of a council meeting.

"I'm sorry, I didn't know about a meeting. I'll be sure to be there, though."

Bess reached across the table and gave Adele's hand a light squeeze.

"We'll be there, too. Point out the movers and shakers around these islands—the people you'll want to get to know better. I'm surprised the sheriff didn't mention the meeting to you."

Adele was wondering the very same thing just as Avery hit the top of the table with the palm of his hand.

"Oh! We should get ourselves a photo of Ripple Island for the front page! Jose, could you take us there this afternoon on your boat?"

Jose shook his head.

"It's in the shop till tomorrow getting a new prop installed, and I have business I need to take care of for the rest of the day."

Adele leaned forward in her chair.

"I have a boat. It's Decklan's runabout. I'm watching it for him while he and Calista are away. It's sitting in my slip at Roche Harbor."

Avery folded his thin arms across his chest and gave a curt nod.

"Then it's settled! I can meet you in Roche at noon, and we'll be on our way. Get there and back before the afternoon winds start to pick up."

Bess waved a finger at her husband.

"You on a little boat like that? I don't think so!"

Avery ground his teeth together. He didn't like being treated like an invalid.

"I'll be fine, Bess. We need the photo for next week's issue and today is as good a day as any. Besides, I really want to get a look at that island up close. I recall it being little more than a big rock. Say, wasn't there some kind of movie filmed out there a while back? Had that famous actor who disappeared in a plane crash somewhere around here. Never found the plane or the body, if I recall. What was his name again?"

Bess's eyes widened.

"Yes, you're right. That had to be almost ten years ago. His name was, uh, Bannister. Brixton Bannister. He won an Oscar for that movie he starred in about the Second World War. Terrible thing about the plane crash. Planes go down in these waters more than we care to admit. Little single-engine things that likely suffer from being piloted with too much bravado and too little required maintenance."

Adele's eyes bounced back and forth between Bess and Avery as they continued their own conversation about a seemingly unrelated subject.

"That's right! One of the greatest actors of our time is what they said after he died. Of course, kind words always seem to come after you're dead. Pity they don't come nearly so often to you when you're still alive. Was the movie they were filming on Ripple Island ever released?"

Bess shook her head.

"No, I don't believe it was. The tabloids at the time reported he was constantly fighting with the director—artistic differences, apparently. Bannister was said to be quite the hothead, all kinds of trouble with the paparazzi, fistfights, rumors of alcoholism. I think there were some who said he might have committed suicide when he crashed his plane into the water. Did I ever tell you I saw him in Roche Harbor when they were filming? He was staying at the hotel there."

Avery's head tilted slightly to the left.

"Really? I don't think you ever mentioned it."

Bess gave Adele a quick wink.

"Well, it's true! A handsome man, I'll tell you that! He was just standing there next to me buying ice cream. I looked up, and there he was! He was very quiet. You could even describe him as shy, painfully shy, but also, oh, I don't know how to say it exactly. There was an energy to him, like the air around him was slightly electrified. He said hello, and I asked him if he was enjoying the islands. I remember he had this thin little smile on his face, like he was thinking of a secret as he was looking around, and then he said in very hushed tones, almost too quiet for me to hear, that he liked them very much. Said it was the kind of place one would be more than happy to never have to leave. And then he walked back into the hotel. I didn't even think to ask for an autograph, stupid old star-struck woman that I was."

Avery appeared horrified at his wife.

"Bess Jenkins, you've been holding out on that encounter all these years? Sharing ice cream moments with handsome Hollywood actors without my knowing? It's enough to make a man feel downright inadequate!"

Bess stood up from the table and then leaned down and kissed Avery on the top of his head.

"Don't worry, husband. I decided not to run away with Brixton Bannister, though I'm pretty sure he was smitten with me. Now you be very careful out on the water today. Make sure the both of you wear your life jackets."

Avery stood up, wincing as his arthritic knees protested the effort.

"I'll be by your slip at noon, Adele, and then we can head out. Until then, by the power of the scone, I declare this staff meeting concluded."

Avery laughed at his own humor and then nudged his wife.

"See? I could have been an actor, too!"

Bess rolled her eyes as she shook her head.

"You could have been *something*, all right."

Adele was smiling to herself while making the short walk back to her car. The sky above was a brilliant blue, the late-morning streets of Friday Harbor fully immersed in the busy bustle of another summer day.

Brixton Bannister.

She vaguely recognized the name and a long-ago story of a missing and eventually declared dead actor, an event that took place before Adele was a teenager. Brixton Bannister, Ripple Island, and a body stuffed into a crab pot and dropped to the bottom of the sea. They were seemingly disparate things, far removed by time, but Adele's keen instincts informed her they might somehow be connected. It was at that moment Adele's mouth fell open as she realized she had failed to ask Sheriff Pine a most obvious question, a failure that left Adele deeply disappointed in herself.

How did the sheriff know to look near Ripple Island for that crab pot? Thousands of acres of water, hundreds of islands, and he somehow knew to look there.

The answer to *that* question was all too clear.

Someone had to have told him where to look.

The soon-to-be journey to Ripple Island suddenly took on far greater importance. It was more than merely a chance to get a photo for a local news article. Adele was determined to see it as an opportunity to possibly provide something far more important.

Answers.

8.

"I wondered when you were going to bring that up."

Avery was behind the wheel of Decklan's runabout. He was initially uncertain about driving the watercraft, not having captained a boat in nearly a decade, but that uncertainty was quickly pushed aside as he took to it with open enthusiasm.

"The only way the sheriff would know to look near Ripple Island was after someone told him to do so. The fact he failed to mention that to you is further evidence he's not telling you everything about what he does and does not know regarding the case. Don't blame him for that. It's his job to keep certain things from the public, especially if those things involve an ongoing murder investigation."

Adele glanced behind her and watched the postcard-like scenery of Roche Harbor fading in the distance as Avery pointed the runabout toward the western tip of neighboring Spieden Island.

"I'm more disappointed in myself for not realizing that sooner. Maybe my solving the case of Calista Stone was nothing more than beginner's luck."

Avery increased the throttle slightly as he shook his head.

"Not likely, my dear. You've a sharp pair of eyes matched to an even sharper mind. Give it a little time, is all."

The runabout's bow skimmed across the remnants of a larger boat's wake, sending a light spray over the windshield. Avery's grin somehow managed to widen even further.

"I forgot how much I enjoy this!"

Adele recalled Decklan Stone having a similar transformation when she first witnessed him driving the same boat. It seemed the combination of water and wind had an unexpectedly powerful, rejuvenating effect on both men.

Avery gave Adele a nudge.

"You care to try?"

Adele considered it for a second or two and then declined the offer.

"No, not yet. For now, I'll just keep watching and learning from you."

The older man shrugged.

"Suit yourself."

The next twenty minutes passed uneventfully as the small craft was ensconced in glasslike waters that gently caressed the rocky shores marking the journey to Ripple Island. Adele looked down at her phone's GPS app and saw they were entering a larger body of water known as Haro Strait. Avery pointed to the right.

"Once we come around Spieden, we'll be into New Channel. Cactus Islands are to the south, and John's Island is to the north. Ripple Island is that big rock about five hundred yards southeast of there. And then that bigger island directly behind John's Island is called Stuart Island."

Adele used her hand to block out the sun's glare as she tried to get a better look at Ripple Island.

"That thing with hardly any trees? That's Ripple Island?"

Avery nodded.

"That's it. Not much to look at, and it's known for having some rather strong currents and a lot of submerged reefs all around it. For the most part, boaters avoid the area. It can't be more than five acres total, no anchorages, and unless you know it better than most, you won't find anywhere to run a little boat like this one onto shore."

Adele glanced at Avery.

"Do *you* know it better than most?"

The old newspaperman's eyes sparkled. He enjoyed teaching Adele more about the area he had called home for so long.

"Yes, indeed I do. It's been a while, but I walked that island some years back, and I'm pretty sure I can recall where we can beach the boat and do it again."

Adele used her phone to snap several pictures of the island and the surrounding area and then stopped as a flash of orange caught her attention.

"What is that?"

Avery's eyes were not nearly as sharp as the much younger Adele's. It took him several more seconds before he was able to spot the buoy floating some seventy yards off Ripple Island's northwest shoreline.

"That appears to be a sheriff's department buoy, so I'd wager that's where they pulled the body from. That would make sense given how they were spotted doing so by those boaters coming back from Canada. They must have been using John's Pass to the north on their way back to Friday Harbor."

Avery slowed the runabout's speed and stood up behind the wheel to better scan the area. His attention was so focused upon that task he hardly felt the shot of pain that blasted through both his knees as he did so.

"I'm pretty sure if we want to get onto the island, we have to move right past that buoy. We're gonna want to take it slow and keep an eye on the depth sounder. Those reefs I was telling you about, they aren't marked. It would be a real sad end to an otherwise beautiful day if we were to get stuck on one."

Adele resumed taking pictures as they slowly approached the dark rock mass that was Ripple Island. The runabout's engine gurgled softly in the background, mingling with the sound of saltwater slapping up against the little island's pockmarked shores. What few trees that grew out from the rock and compacted earth were small, shriveled pretenders of their big island counterparts. Even bathed in the warm light of the afternoon sun, the island had an undeniably ominous aura to it, like that quiet voice in one's head that warns of potential danger.

"It's depressing."

Avery was about to nod his head in agreement when he turned the boat sharply to the left.

"Damn, almost did it."

Adele noted a parade of ripples that covered a forty-by-forty area of water.

"Did what?"

"See those ripples? That's a reef just under the surface. Now you know where the island gets its name. We hit that, lose a prop, and it's drifting time for us—no power."

They passed the bright-orange sheriff's department buoy. Adele took a picture of it and then turned her attention back to Ripple Island. There appeared to be no beach they could drive the runabout onto. It was all inhospitable, steep, rugged rock.

"You sure you had a way to get yourself onto the island?"

Avery's eyes widened in exaggerated shock.

"Are you inferring my memory isn't what it used to be, Ms. Plank?"

Adele chuckled.

"I'm just wondering, is all."

Avery jabbed a finger toward a lighter section of the rocky shore.

"Ah-ha! There it is! You'll see. There's a little sandy beach right around the corner."

Adele was glad to find Avery's memory proved correct. A narrow opening between two fragmented fingers of rock revealed the very beach he was certain would be found. With a slight bump of the throttle from Avery, the runabout's bow pushed up onto the sandy surface. He tilted the outboard upward to keep the prop from digging into the beach. Avery offered Adele a section of white rope and pointed to a scraggly shrub growing twenty feet from the confluence of beach and water.

"If you could tie us off so Mr. Stone's boat doesn't end up floating away with the tide, we'll be good to go."

Adele took another picture, grabbed the rope, stepped over the small windshield, and then hopped down onto the beach. After reaching the dark-green shrub, she bent down to wrap the rope around its base and then stopped. Avery noticed the pause and called out from behind her.

"Is everything OK?"

Adele ran her hand along the shrub's small trunk and found it abnormally worn and smooth. Lying on the sand next to it were a few short strands of light-yellow fiber. She picked them up and placed them into her pocket before continuing to tie the runabout to the shrub.

"Got it!"

Avery made his way slowly across the beach until he stood next to Adele.

"What were you looking at?"

Adele pointed at the shrub.

"I think someone else has been tying up here like we just did."

Avery leaned forward and ran his hand along the bottom of the shrub's worn wood surface. What he felt caused him to grunt.

"You're right. For the wood at the bottom of that trunk to get as smooth as it is requires a lot of use, *years* of having a rope tied and untied to it. Who in the hell would be doing that on this god-forsaken rock? And *why*? There's nothing here."

Adele began to navigate what appeared to be little more than a hint of a trail in the rock and sand that led away from the tiny cove. She stopped to look behind her, realizing Avery might be unable to follow.

"You go on ahead, young lady. My bones aren't up for any kind of hike. Just be careful."

Adele moved up the trail and then turned around. She could see the runabout on the beach, as well as the water on all sides surrounding the small island. The trail led to a cluster of thin, sickly-looking pine trees that grew out from a small patch if earth, their trunks bent from decades of wind. The ground smelled of bird droppings, dirt, and dry grass.

The trail then extended toward the island's northern side. Adele followed it carefully. Her eyes scanned the ground for any clue that might suggest who put the trail there in the first place.

She found none, and soon the trail disappeared altogether, dropping down between another narrow break in the rocks that lead to a shallow, seemingly unmoving pool of water. The water extended some thirty feet beyond where Adele stood staring at a thick shrub and wall of rock on the opposite side.

After taking a few more photos of the area, she retraced her steps until she was once again looking out from Ripple Island's near-barren pinnacle. The sound of a speeding boat was carried upon the wind. Adele peered out with narrowed eyes, searching for the source of the noise until she spotted the thirty-foot dark-blue blur skipping across the small waves a thousand yards to the northeast. Its long wake indicated it had come from Canada and was now making its way toward President Channel and the northeastern shores of Orcas Island. The vessel suddenly veered right, altering its course so it was coming directly toward Ripple Island. The boat was both unusually fast and loud, courtesy of its side-hull exhaust. Adele estimated it to be traveling at nearly fifty miles an hour. Its long-nosed bow easily dissected the water in front of it as its speed increased even more.

Adele moved behind the small cluster of trees, hoping to keep out of sight while watching the vessel's rapid approach with curious trepidation. The roar of the dual inboard motors filled Adele's ears, drowning out everything else around her. She snapped a couple more pictures, noting the outline of two men standing behind the boat's darkened glass windshield but was unable to clearly see their faces. Without slowing, the boat blasted past the sheriff's department buoy, avoiding it by just a few yards before abruptly turning and speeding off. Only after the vessel was little more than a spec on the horizon did Adele move out from behind the trees.

A short time later she found Avery standing on the beach watching her return. He pointed out at the water.

"That was certainly interesting, eh?"

Adele nodded. She handed Avery her phone to show him the pictures she had just taken.

"Do you recognize the boat? I'm pretty sure it had two men onboard, but I couldn't make out their faces."

Avery shook his head.

"No. It was *loud*. I couldn't see it from the beach here, but I damn sure heard it."

"Do you think they saw you or the runabout?"

Again, Avery shook his head.

"I don't think so. They would have had to know how to get here to see me. They just sort of roared on by. You able to see anything that might indicate what they were doing here?"

"They went right past the buoy, like they wanted to get a good look at it. And I'm pretty certain the boat came in from across the border."

Avery glanced down at his watch.

"Well, for now we'll just add that boat to our wait and see file. Maybe mention it to the sheriff and see what he says. Until then, we better start making our way back to Roche if we're going to make tonight's council meeting in Friday Harbor. The tide is starting to go out again. You think you're ready to do the driving?"

Though she was nervous, Adele gave the old man a confident nod.

"Sure, no better way of learning than actually doing, right?"

Avery nudged Adele's shoulder.

"That's the spirit!"

They untied the rope attached to the shrub. Adele used an oar to push the boat backward off the beach. Once that was accomplished, she lowered the prop into the water, started the outboard, and then bumped it into reverse a few times before putting it into forward gear and slowly moving into deeper water, making certain to avoid the areas where ripples hinted at reefs hiding just beneath the surface.

Soon, they were crossing New Channel and nearing Spieden Island. Adele gripped the wheel tightly, battling equal parts nervousness and exhilaration. She finally understood the appeal of captaining a boat, however small, over water and around islands. She thought perhaps there was something of the explorer in all of us. That yearning to set out into the unknown, a deep-rooted human motivation to discover the undiscovered not only among our surroundings, but, perhaps more importantly, within ourselves. She was reminded of a line from Herman Melville's *Moby Dick*.

"It is not down in any map; true places never are."

Avery stood up from the passenger seat, pointing at something directly in front of them.

"Slow down!"

Adele was about to ask what Avery saw when it revealed itself to her in all its glistening black-and-white predatory glory. The tip of the dark dorsal fin extended upward nearly five feet as it broke the water's surface. The orca whale's massive head gently lifted out of the water before gracefully plunging back below the surface in a nearly silent gesture that belied the great power of the beast.

"The male leads the pod. Look, there's at least four more right behind him. The female dorsal fins are much smaller."

Adele stared wide-eyed at the leisurely parade of whales as they swam no more than forty feet past the runabout, their passage causing waves to rock the boat from side to side.

"You might want to hold on."

Adele was quick to detect the hint of concern in Avery's voice. She located the source of that trepidation. A six-foot-tall dorsal fin marked the approach of an even larger male orca. Unlike the others in the pod, though, this one appeared intent on getting an even closer look at the boat and its occupants.

"He's not going to hit us, is he?"

Avery stared at the whale's deliberate path toward the runabout.

"Like I said, hold on. And you might want to get a picture or two while you're at it."

The air just above the great sea mammal erupted in a whooshing cloud of mist as he expelled a breath. His upper half curled downward and then the rest of the long, wide body followed until the tip of his tail disappeared beneath the water with a soft slap. With the whale seemingly gone, Adele wondered why Avery still appeared so tense. The old man's mouth was a tight-lipped scowl as his eyes continued to scan the watery surface surrounding the little boat. The cries of screeching seagulls echoed across the channel.

"Oh!"

Adele instinctively flinched as a mass of white moved directly underneath her. The male orca had rolled onto his back to avoid hitting the boat with his dorsal fin. Adele locked eyes with the creature. She stared into the dark orbs, and found herself immobile, utterly awestruck by the display. The sea mammal's eyes were curious, even playful. Adele would have sworn he winked at her.

At the very moment she took a picture, the orca's tail bumped the bottom of the boat, making a deep, scraping thump as he did so. He then dived deeper and was gone as quickly as he had appeared.

Adele looked down to find a pair of badly shaking hands holding her phone. Her head turned and there was Avery grinning at her. Whatever momentary fear he had indicated earlier was gone.

"*That* is something you'll remember for the rest of your life!"

Adele took a deep breath and managed to smile back while trying to force her hands to stop shaking.

"You read about how big those things are, but to see them up close? Man, they're *huge*!"

They both settled back down slowly into their seats. Avery was still smiling.

"I've had people tell me about orcas swimming under them, but I never saw it myself—until today. This was your first time driving a boat out in these waters, Adele. Think about that. I know people who've lived all their lives in these islands, out on the water day after day for years, and never had that kind of experience. And here you are, already witness to one of the most remarkable interactions between human and whale a person can have. I'd say these islands like you—*a lot*."

Adele put the runabout in gear and pushed the throttle forward until it was on plane and speeding back toward Roche Harbor. The slight sting of the saltwater air against her face helped to clear her head and dissipate the fear that had accompanied the visit by the pod of orcas. She wondered if there was any truth to Avery's words. Was it possible for a physical place to extend a greeting to those seeking both a purpose and a home?

Perhaps the islands *did* like her. If so, the feeling was mutual.

9.

Sitting in the small, low-ceilinged space that was the San Juan County council chambers located inside a nondescript two-story gray local government building in Friday Harbor, Adele was reminded of a remark by former US congressman Tip O'Neill, a colorful twentieth-century Irish American with a penchant for saying little while saying much: All politics is local.

The forty-by-forty room was dominated by the semicircular desk at the front occupied by the three current members of the San Juan County Council. Two were middle-aged men, and one was a heavy-set woman of similar age. At the end of the table on the left side of the room was Sheriff Pine. He appeared slightly nervous at the gathering of nearly twenty locals. According to Bess, that was easily double the number who typically attended the monthly meetings.

"Compared to a normal meeting, this is a full house. Folks are wondering about that body that was found, and it'll be our job to report the facts. Council business is always an easy story, and people like to read about it—even the boring stuff like building permits, utility fees, and such. But a murder investigation, well, that's something else entirely."

Adele glanced at the assortment of faces behind her. Most were older with the exception of a younger man who sat at the very back. He was dressed in a dark-blue sweater with the sleeves rolled up and white cargo shorts. His well-tanned unlined face had the look of someone utterly content in their own skin.

"Hello, and welcome to this evening's council meeting. We have a rather large crowd here tonight, so I'll ask that those wishing to provide public comments do so while keeping in mind others may wish to speak as well. We don't want to be here too long, as we all have families we'd like to get back home to."

Adele jotted down the name of the councilman who started the meeting.

Roger Wilcox.

She then did the same for the two other council members, reading from the name tags placed in front of them.

Joe Box. Sandra Plume. A thin, older woman stood up from her plastic chair and cleared her throat. She wore a purple sweater-vest, light-blue turtleneck shirt, and loose-fitting jeans pulled up high above her narrow waist.

"Please state your name and address for the record."

The woman gave Councilman Wilcox a scowl.

"You know who I am, Roger."

The councilman, who had a fleshy face and naturally ruddy complexion, nodded.

"Yes, I do, but it's for the record. Please state your name and address, and then you can make your public comment."

The woman looked back at the other residents and rolled her eyes at them before returning her attention to the council.

"Everything these days is so formal, like a bunch of kids playing grown-up! My name is Constance Baker. I live out on Bayview Drive, the old yellow house with the rose garden out front. You all know it."

Councilman Wilcox attempted to give Constance a reassuring smile, but she appeared to refuse the gesture and instead pointed at Sheriff Pine.

"I suppose I'm here tonight like all the rest. I want to know about that body you found out by Ripple Island. Was it a murder? That's what some people are saying, but I'd rather hear the facts from you, Lucas, instead of relying on rumors."

The young sheriff folded his hands together and shifted in his chair.

"It's an ongoing investigation, Mrs. Baker. I can confirm there was a body found in the water recently. At this time, I am not at liberty to say more."

Avery leaned in closer to Adele so he could whisper into her ear.

"Constance Baker is still teaching at the primary school. Been there for over forty years. She's had thousands of island kids come through her classroom door, including everyone sitting behind that desk."

"Don't you try to play games with me, Lucas Pine. I'm happy to see a good local boy wearing that badge, and I've known your family for longer than I can remember, but if there's been a murder, we have a right to know about it."

Lucas glanced at the members of the council, and then gave his former school teacher a shrug.

"I'm sorry, Mrs. Baker. Until I have more information, I cannot comment further on this matter."

Adele wasn't sure why she did what she did at that moment. She just did.

"Perhaps the sheriff can explain how he came to know the exact location of where the body was found?"

Every pair of eyes in the room stared back at Adele, including those of Sheriff Pine, whose jaw clenched repeatedly as he glared at the newly arrived news reporter and recent guest at his home. If he had thought sharing a burger and beers with Adele would be enough to keep her from putting him on the spot, she had just proved that assumption wrong.

Before Lucas could try to answer, Avery stood up and introduced her to those attending the council meeting.

"For those who might not already know, this is Adele Plank. She's working for the paper. You likely read her story last year on the writer and his wife, Mr. and Mrs. Stone, and all that mess with the former sheriff."

A soft murmur worked its way through the room. Constance Baker pointed at Adele and then jabbed a finger in the sheriff's direction.

"That story has a lot to do with this, too, Sheriff. We're all pulling for you, but when you're wearing that badge, well, there are some of us who might not be ready to trust you just yet. I know for a fact some folks want the sheriff's department to be disbanded and to hand over island law enforcement to the state police. We don't pay your salary to be lied to, young man. So maybe you could answer Ms. Plank's question. How did you know where to find that body out in the middle of all that water?"

Lucas's eyes flashed the betrayal he felt at Adele for having pitted him against his own people. The tips of the fingers of his folded hands that he rested atop the desk were white as he clenched them tightly together.

"I'll have more information, including the nature of how we came to locate the body in question, soon, Mrs. Baker."

Adele cleared her throat.

"Should I take that as a no comment, Sheriff Pine?"

Eyes widened as people watched the verbal battle being waged between sheriff and reporter.

"I believe I told you personally there would be an official statement delivered to your newspaper soon, Ms. Plank. Until then, I cannot comment further on the matter."

Another round of whispered murmurs moved across the meeting room, most of which appeared to disagree with the sheriff's refusal to say anything more definitive about the case of the recently discovered body.

"Councilman Wilcox, might I have a few words?"

The murmurs abruptly ceased as the man Adele had earlier spotted sitting in the back of the room made his way to the front. He was nearly six feet tall, with a lean, muscular body that made clear he spent considerable time keeping himself in shape. His short dark-brown hair was parted neatly to the side, and when he smiled, a row of perfectly aligned, brilliant-white teeth were revealed.

But his eyes don't smile.

Councilman Wilcox appeared all too eager to allow the younger man to speak.

"By all means, Mr. Soros, I'm sure we're all interested in what you have to say regarding this matter."

Bess's face tightened as if she had just smelled something bad.

"That's Roland Soros, the grandson of Charles Soros who started the first local bank here in Friday Harbor. Nothing more than a spoiled brat, if you ask me. Been trying to buy our office building the last few years so he can put up more waterfront condos. At first we told him no thank you. Now we just tell him to go to hell. There's not a one of those council members sitting up there who isn't already in his pocket."

Roland's voice was deeper than his years would suggest and indicative of his absolute confidence in anything and everything he might wish to say to others.

"As you all know, I was instrumental in bringing Sheriff Pine back to our islands. I knew he would do a good job and restore both trust and confidence in our local law enforcement. What he is doing is what professionals must do in such cases: gather facts, deliberate, and then release information to the public only when it is appropriate to do so. We're in the middle of tourist season. The last thing our local businesses need is to have a sheriff's department, if you'll pardon the expression, shooting from the hip about a dead body. I have every confidence in our sheriff and just wanted to take a moment to make that clear—to *all* of you."

Roland nodded to the sheriff. Lucas nodded back clearly grateful for the support. Councilman Wilcox cleared his throat loudly before proceeding.

"I think I speak for the rest of the council when I commend Mr. Soros for his comments. He's right. We need to allow the sheriff time to do the job we hired him to do."

The other two members of the council sat silent, their eyes fixated on the table in front of them as if weighted down by some unspoken shame.

After that, the council meeting resumed its normal course of business as outlined by the agenda. There were brief discussions of park fees, the need to repave a portion of road on the southern end of the island, and a bid review for roof repairs to the county courthouse. By the time people were filing out of the meeting, they appeared largely bored by the proceedings, the brief back and forth between Adele and the sheriff all but forgotten. Avery and Bess had already left for home, both tired and ready for bed.

"Excuse me, Ms. Plank, might I have a word?"

Adele turned around to find Roland Soros looking down at her as they both stood on the sidewalk outside. The air was warm and remnants of daylight still remained despite it being nearly ten o'clock in the evening.

Roland held out his hand and lightly shook Adele's.

"I just wanted to introduce myself. I recall reading your article on the writer and his wife and found it very good. Even more impressive was how you managed to solve the mystery of Mrs. Stone's disappearance so quickly."

"Thank you, Mr. Soros."

Roland flashed his well-practiced smile.

"Please, call me Roland. Now I know I'm not a favorite of Avery and Bess, but I am a supporter of having a local newspaper and am especially happy to see that they've hired some new blood. That's a very good thing, and, dare I say, much needed."

Adele smiled but said nothing, sensing Roland had yet to fully reveal the intent of his having requested to speak with her.

"Perhaps you would like to have dinner tomorrow? I would love to sit down and discuss potential business opportunities involving the paper, advertising, and whatnot. Anything I can do to help it remain a viable part of the community."

Adele heard the sound of heavy footsteps approaching from behind her and then saw the tall form of Lucas Pine as the sheriff reached out to shake Roland's hand.

"Thanks for the support, Roland. It's appreciated. As for you, Ms. Plank . . ."

Adele's eyes narrowed.

"*What*? I have a job to do, Sheriff. I told you that already."

"And I told you I would be sending an official statement for the paper as soon as possible. I don't appreciate being sideswiped at a public council meeting."

Adele let out a snort that was louder than she intended.

"That wasn't a sideswipe. That was a simple question about a matter of public importance. I'm a reporter. You're the sheriff. That means sometimes I'm going to have to ask you questions you might not want to answer. If that bothers you so much, maybe you're not cut out for the job."

As soon as she spoke the words, Adele regretted them. She knew there was a difference between aggressive reporting and rudeness and feared she had just participated in the latter.

"Uh, Ms. Plank, perhaps we should schedule dinner for another time?"

Lucas's brows rose as his eyes darted from Adele to Roland and then back to Adele.

"Dinner?"

"Yes, I offered to have dinner with Ms. Plank to discuss business related to the newspaper."

The sheriff's posture straightened until he stood at his full height. He looked down at both Adele and Roland and then gave a curt nod.

"OK, I see. Well, then, enjoy your dinner, Ms. Plank. I'm sure it'll be better than the beer and burgers you had at my place."

Roland held up his hands in front of him.

"Hey, I didn't know you two were—"

Adele cut him off.

"We're *not*, Mr. Soros. And I'd be happy to sit down with you. Just give me a time and place."

"There's the Gooseberry Inn halfway between here and Roche Harbor. Does eight o'clock tomorrow night work?"

Adele smiled as she nodded, ignoring the sheriff's tight-jawed stare.

"That'll be just fine. See you then."

Lucas rested his right hand on the butt of his revolver as both he and Adele watched Roland walk across the street toward his black four-door Mercedes.

"You watch yourself. That man might appear to be all smiles and good intentions, but he's a shark and has been known to bite those who cross him."

"He seems to support you well enough, Sheriff Pine."

Lucas's response was limited to just one word.

"Yeah."

And with that, the sheriff began to move away from Adele. After a few long-legged strides, he paused and turned around.

"I'll get you that press release soon. Enjoy your dinner with Roland, Ms. Plank."

Adele wanted to say something in response but remained mute, a prisoner to her own conflicted emotions. She was angry with Lucas for his anger with her, but also felt bad for having made him feel so defensive of the job he was doing as sheriff. And then there was the matter of her just-scheduled dinner with Roland Soros. Rich, young, and good-looking were hardly qualities to be ignored, and Adele had to admit she found the local businessman attractive.

Then again, she found Lucas Pine equally attractive.

Decisions, decisions. . .

10.

"Oh, my goodness! This is delicious!"

Roland was clearly pleased by how much Adele was enjoying her meal inside the rustic Gooseberry Inn restaurant, where they were seated at a private table in the back corner of the dimly lit dining room located adjacent to a small pond that sat back some two hundred yards from the main road.

She took another bite of the glazed duck breast, closed her eyes, and smiled, an act that caused Roland to chuckle.

"I told you—best on the island. My grandparents used to bring me here on my birthday."

Normally, Adele would never have ordered something so expensive, but Roland insisted, reminding her more than once that the meal was his treat.

During the first twenty minutes of their dinner meeting, Adele had managed to coax a bit of personal information out of the island businessman. She discovered his parents had died in an auto accident when he was just five. They were living in Florida at the time. Roland's grandparents took him in, brought him back with them to the San Juans, and raised him from then on in their expansive water-view Friday Harbor home.

"After a few years, the pain and confusion over losing my parents diminished, though it never went away entirely. My grandfather taught me discipline and the benefits of hard work, while my grandmother gave me encouragement and love. All in all, it was a good childhood. I never wanted for anything and was allowed to take our little aluminum fishing boat out whenever I wanted. I must have logged thousands of hours on these waters. I explored every nook and cranny I could find and fished and crabbed all along the way. It really is a remarkable place to grow up."

"Still, to lose your parents at such a young age—it must have been difficult."

Roland tore the corner off a freshly made sourdough roll and dipped it into the remnants of the crab bisque he had ordered.

"Yeah, I suppose there were elements of isolation at times. I was a bit withdrawn, socially awkward. Being on the water was my escape. It also made me tougher than the other kids, more determined to succeed. I might have grown up with money, but most of them got to grow up with both their parents.

"I know there are some people around here who want to judge me for having been given the proverbial silver spoon, but while I had certain advantages, I've made it a point to use them to their fullest. I want to bring these islands into the modern era, make them a thriving, forward-focused enterprise. I see no reason why we can't continue to respect this area's past while also expanding the potential for a greater economic future."

Adele found it difficult to imagine the current version of Roland Soros to be a withdrawn, socially awkward youth. He oozed such comfortable confidence that it bordered on outright bravado.

"You sound like a politician."

Roland flinched as he shook his head.

"Oh, god, I hope not! No, I have no need to be something I can easily buy."

Adele's fork paused at the halfway point between plate and mouth. She found the choice of words interesting and with multiple potential implications.

"You buy politicians?"

Roland took a deep breath.

"Ah, perhaps I should have said it differently. Let's just say that as someone with multiple ventures, a man who is responsible for the livelihoods of a good many people, I make certain to maintain a degree of influence or at the very least to have a seat at the table when necessary."

"Does that include Sheriff Pine?"

Sensing the trap Adele was setting for him, Roland was quick to attempt a verbal pivot.

"Don't let that duck get too cold. It's best when warm."

"And don't *you* avoid the question, Mr. Soros. How much influence do you have with Lucas? Don't worry. This is all off the record."

Roland lowered his fork to his plate next to what little remained of the baked halibut that accompanied his bisque and looked into Adele's eyes for several silent seconds.

"I think Lucas will make a great sheriff. We grew up together, you know. I was two classes ahead of him, but he was much more popular, being an athlete and all. His family has been an integral part of these islands, and I am determined to keep our local law enforcement just that—*local*."

"You're still not answering my question. Does your relationship with Lucas come with a certain degree of influence and if so how much?"

Roland shrugged.

"We're two relatively young men who grew up in the same place as kids. Beyond that, Lucas is his own man, and I respect that."

"And that's it?"

"Yeah, that's it. Now let's talk about that newspaper of yours. I know of at least three area businesses that aren't advertising with you yet. I'd be happy to make a few calls and get them on board. It would provide a nice little boost to the bottom line."

Adele took the last bite of duck and then folded her arms across her chest.

"That is a discussion you should be having with Avery and Bess. My job right now is to investigate and write stories. It's their newspaper, not mine."

Roland wagged a finger at Adele.

"Don't sell yourself short. Avery and Bess are fine people, more stubborn than most, but fine people. That said, theirs is a world that is all but gone. You represent the paper's future. People know your name. They know your ability to get to the truth. I have no doubt the readers will be identifying it as *your* paper soon enough, and I also have no doubt both Avery and Bess are aware of that fact. It's likely why they seem so willing to bring you on board. If they don't get someone to take over, the paper will possibly die off like so many other businesses have around here. Stagnation leads to irrelevance, and the *Island Gazette* has been mired in its own irrelevance for quite some time."

The waiter, an older silver-haired man dressed in black slacks and a crisp white dress shirt, approached their table to ask if everything was OK. Roland waved him away and then continued to speak to Adele, his chest leaning forward over the table as he did so.

"There's always potential with news media, Adele. The *Island Gazette* has a name that resonates with the longtime residents. That's an asset, but it also needs to start reaching out to the younger, upwardly mobile demographic. That's where I can help. New advertising clients, a monetized website, and that's just a start. You could be making a comfortable living within a year or two, and, most important, be your own boss. Your news, your deadlines, *your* newspaper."

Before Adele could respond, Roland interjected.

"No need to answer right now. Keep learning from Avery and Bess, get to know the community better, the people who will talk and those who would rather not. But at the same time keep my offer in mind. I think you'd be a good fit for this place."

"Why?"

Roland's eyes narrowed.

"What do you mean?"

It was Adele's turn to lean forward and try to hold Roland's gaze with her own.

"Why are you going to the trouble of giving someone you hardly know a business opportunity?"

Roland's mouth curled upward into a half grin.

"You mean to ask what's in it for me, am I right?"

Adele shrugged.

"I won't say I'm *not* wondering about that very thing."

"Fair enough. The fact is I *do* know you by reputation and now somewhat personally. I like what I see. These islands need a more forward-thinking, more progressive newspaper. I have big plans for this place, plans that will bring in hundreds more jobs, grow the economy, improve our schools, services, and, ultimately, our way of life."

"And you think it would make your plans more acceptable to the public if you had the local newspaper regularly explaining your version of things."

Roland cocked his head and grunted.

"You don't miss much, do you? You're every bit as observant as I suspected. I'll admit it—having someone besides Avery and Bess to tell my side of things would be a big help. In the end, though, you are free to report how you see it, Adele. I can't put words into your mouth, and I wouldn't try. All I am asking of you right now is to consider the possibility of taking charge of the newspaper in the not too distant future. Bess and Avery aren't getting any younger."

Adele raised her water glass.

"Well, here's to consideration of possibilities, then."

Roland gave an approving smile and raised his glass as well.

"To a mutually beneficial future for the both of us."

A short time later, Roland was slowly walking Adele to her car in the gravel parking lot outside the restaurant. They said nothing while their shoes made soft crunching noises as they moved across the compacted stones.

Adele, with her keys in hand, turned toward Roland. She found him pleasant, interesting, and intelligent but wasn't yet sure if she liked him in any way other than merely as a friendly acquaintance, though it seemed there might be potential for something more.

"Thank you for the dinner. It was very good."

Roland flashed another smile as he stood with both hands stuffed into the front pockets of his khakis. The pink hue of his golf shirt was partially illuminated by the half-moon that peeked out from the gathering of evening clouds overhead.

"It was my pleasure, Adele. I hope we can do it again soon. You're staying on Delroy Hicks's old sailboat in Roche, isn't that right?"

Adele nodded.

"Yes."

"I keep a boat there at the marina as well. It's a 1959 Burger that was first purchased by my grandfather many, many years ago."

Adele knew the boat. She had walked past its gleaming white hull and yards of glossy teak railings several times already while exploring the other parts of the marina.

"That's not a boat. It's a yacht! You own that?"

Roland nodded.

"Like I said, it was in the family long before I inherited it. The marina staff has someone who keeps it maintained for me. I actually haven't stepped foot on it in months. Can never seem to find the time. I thought of selling it, but it has sentimental value, and it's only been a few years since my grandfather passed, so I keep holding on to her for now. I'd be happy to show you inside, give you the tour, if you like."

Adele surprised herself by how quickly she accepted.

"Sure, that would be great."

Roland nodded.

"Very good, then. It's a date."

The word *date* lingered in silence far longer than either Adele or Roland would have liked.

"Thank you again, Roland. Drive home safe."

"You, too, Adele. Take care, and please remember to think over what I said regarding the newspaper."

Once Adele was back behind the wheel of her MINI, she took a moment to make certain her rearview mirror was properly adjusted. It was then she saw Roland standing next to his Mercedes speaking with a tall, broad-shouldered man whose face was completely hidden within a dark hoodie. She could hear the man hissing angry words at Roland and then Roland telling him to keep his voice down.

Because he doesn't want me to hear what they're talking about.

The stranger's voice grew louder as the man gave Roland a hard shove, causing his back to slam up against the side of the Mercedes. Adele rolled down her window, hoping to hear what was being said.

"That's not how things work around here, Sergei. Give me another forty-eight hours."

"We already give you forty-eight hours. We give you three days. We give you three weeks. No more giving!"

Roland leaned closer to the man he called Sergei and whispered something Adele couldn't hear. Both men then turned to stare directly at Adele's car, which remained parked just fifty feet from where they stood.

A mass of clouds crept across the sky, blocking out what little moonlight remained, plunging the parking lot into almost total darkness. Adele suddenly had the overwhelming urge to be anywhere but there. She scrambled to place her key into the ignition while the sound of approaching footsteps sounded a warning that sent her survival instincts into overdrive.

With the car started, she slammed it into gear and popped the clutch, sending a spray of gravel shooting out from behind the little vehicle as it sped away from the restaurant. Right before turning onto the paved road, she looked into the rearview mirror and saw the dark form of the man in the hoodie running to try to catch up to the car. Adele was certain she saw the outline of a gun in his right hand.

Her foot slammed down on the gas pedal, causing the tires to chirp as the MINI hit the pavement at nearly forty miles an hour and then continued to accelerate from there. Normally, it would have been a leisurely ten-minute drive back to Roche Harbor. Adele made it there in just over five.

She found a well-lit area to park her car. Only after making certain she hadn't been followed did she remove her key and step outside into the warm summer evening air. Laughter echoed across the resort from one of the docks on the west side, and the bright lights of occupied vessels shined across the entirety of the marina. It was a three hundred–yard walk to the safety of her sailboat.

I wasn't followed. There are lots of people around. I'm OK. Besides, I have no idea who that man was or if he actually intended to do me any harm. Fact is I kind of freaked out, didn't I?

With a final glance behind her, Adele turned to make her way toward the marina entrance when she froze, her eyes fixed upon a small area on the back-right corner of her car just below the taillight. Her fingers trembled as they traced the rough outline of the metal indentation. She forced herself to take slow, deep breaths, not believing what her eyes told her to be true.

It was a bullet hole.

11.

"Well?"

Sheriff Pine shined his flashlight at the back of Adele's car and peered closely at the same hole she had just recently discovered. She had called Lucas from inside her sailboat and then ventured back out to her car only after Lucas called her back on his cell phone telling her he had arrived at the Roche Harbor parking lot.

"It definitely looks to be from a bullet. So you believe it was fired by a man named Sergei who was speaking with Roland Soros outside the Gooseberry Inn?"

Adele nodded and then told the sheriff more of her story. She gave a description of the man in the hoodie, the heated words between him and Roland, and how he followed her car as it pulled out of the restaurant parking lot.

"But you didn't see this Sergei's face?"

"No, it was dark and he had most of it covered inside the hood. He had a thick accent. Russian, I think."

Adele tried to stop her body from trembling but found she couldn't.

"It's OK, Ms. Plank, I'm here. You did the right thing in calling me."

Lucas bent over to look at the bullet hole once again.

"Given your description of how close he was to the back of your car, the man is either a very bad shot or this was meant as some kind of warning."

"A warning about what?"

The sheriff shrugged.

"That's what I intend to find out. I'll be questioning Roland, uh, Mr. Soros, first thing in the morning."

Adele found her shaking had finally ceased—the result of Lucas's calming presence.

"Is Roland a suspect?"

"No, for now I'd merely consider him a witness. Now you said you overheard this Sergei tell Roland that he wasn't going to give him any more time, is that right?"

Adele nodded.

"Yeah, that's *exactly* what he said."

A young couple passed under a street lamp on the other side of the parking lot on their way to the hotel. They paused to look at the sheriff standing next to Adele before resuming their walk. Similar to the previous day, Adele again had the sensation of being watched. She didn't want to be alone. Lucas sensed her apprehension.

"I'll walk you back to your boat and then hang around here for a while, OK?"

"No, I can't ask that of you, Sheriff. You need to get back home. It's late, your father—"

Lucas waved off Adele's concerns.

"Dad will be sleeping until morning, and even then he has his routine and doesn't need me there. I'm not tired, and if someone followed you back here, they'll find me waiting for them. Think of it as a bit of police protection, and that's just me doing my job. C'mon, let's get you home."

Adele allowed the sheriff to rest his hand gently against her shoulders as they made their way back to the sailboat. She liked feeling its weight on her, a hint of the physical strength Lucas possessed. Though she prided herself on being a strong, independent young woman, Adele wasn't so proud as to deny herself the momentary opportunity to feel protected.

"I'll be right outside. You get some sleep."

"Can I get you something to drink or eat?"

The sheriff shook his head.

"No, thank you, I'm fine. Just try and get some rest."

Once inside the well-protected fiberglass shell of her new home, Adele took a moment to peek out between the porthole curtains and look upon the tall, still form of Sheriff Pine standing alone on the dock cloaked in near darkness. She knew her eyes lingered on his body for longer than they should, but she didn't care. She liked what she saw.

Adele lay down in bed but didn't think she would be able to fall asleep, still too rattled that someone had likely fired a gun at her. And yet sleep did eventually take her, allowing for several hours of much-needed rest.

When she awoke, she was stunned to find the sheriff still standing on the dock outside her boat, just as he had been doing when she last saw him the night before. Her phone indicated it was just after six in the morning. With a soft groan, she pushed herself back onto her feet. She opened the door and stepped onto the dock, rubbing the sleep from her eyes as she did so.

"I can't believe you stood out here all night. I feel terrible. You must be so tired. Can I make you some coffee?"

Lucas shook his head, appearing remarkably alert given he was running on no sleep.

"No thanks. I'm heading back to Friday Harbor to speak with Roland. That is, unless you're still feeling scared about last night."

Though she knew he meant well, Adele didn't like Lucas thinking she was too afraid to be alone, especially with daylight having returned.

"I'm OK. You go do your job and then get some rest. And maybe you could give me an update on what you find out?"

The sheriff scratched the light stubble on his cheek and then nodded.

"You bet. I'll check in with you this afternoon. Oh, and the newspaper should be receiving the official statement today as well from the sheriff's office regarding the body we found. Until then, if you need anything, don't hesitate to call."

Lucas readied himself to turn around and walk away but hesitated, seeming to struggle with something more he wanted to say before leaving.

"What is it?"

The sheriff's eyes looked down at his feet.

"I just wanted you to know that I normally wouldn't have spent all night keeping guard in front of a residence. Maybe an hour or two, but not all night. I was happy to make an exception for you. I'm no banker or businessman, I don't own buildings or yachts, but if we were to get to know each other better, and if we find there's something there worth knowing, I damn sure would keep you safe."

Adele watched Lucas wince as soon as he said the words. He shut his eyes tight and shook his head before quickly attempting to diffuse what he thought to have been a mistake.

"I'm sorry, that was too much, wasn't it? There was a time around here people thought me quite the ladies' man, but I'm pretty sure those days are long gone. It's just, uh, you had that dinner date with Roland, and I felt like I might be missing my chance to get to know you better, and I really *would* like to get to know you better, Adele."

"I feel the same, Lucas, but I'm not looking for a relationship, so let's just call ourselves friends for now and see what happens."

The sheriff looked up into the brightening San Juan Islands morning sky before abruptly dropping his chin down onto his chest.

"Uh-oh, are you putting me into the friend room, Ms. Plank?"

Adele smiled, trying to reassure Lucas she did in fact find him attractive.

"I promise it's not a room I see myself locking the door on. In fact, I'm open to having you take me out sometime if you like."

The sheriff gave a quick nod and then turned around. His footsteps thumped against the dock as his voice carried back to Adele, who remained standing next to her boat.

"It's a date, then. I'll be in touch, Ms. Plank."

Adele followed Lucas's departure, silently marveling at how after years of wandering aimlessly in the near-barren relationship desert, she was now being pursued by two vastly different yet equally handsome and interesting men. And then she frowned as she remembered that her dinner date with Roland ended in a mysterious stranger apparently firing a gun into the back of her car.

You never make it simple on yourself, do you Adele? That would make quite a story for the kids. I could tell them about how the first time I had dinner with their dad a man shot at me. Yeah, that sounds just great.

Adele withdrew her hand from a front pocket and looked down to see it holding the remnants of yellow rope she had taken from the beach on Ripple Island. She glanced around the marina and found it still blanketed by the quiet stillness of early morning, interrupted only by the strident call of seagulls flying overhead.

It was time to take a walk before the resort once again resumed the busy bustle of another tourist season day.

For the next thirty minutes, Adele moved down one dock and then another and yet another, until finally she stood looking at a row of small craft tied up to guest moorage near the fuel dock at the marina's entrance. It was an assortment of dinghy-size boats, some new, some old, and one that appeared to have possibly been abandoned. It was a twelve-foot fiberglass skiff with a hull deeply gouged by years of water-journey abuse. The floor of its interior had several inches of dark, dank seawater upon which floated small bits of debris. On the back hung an old, oil-encrusted two-stroke motor, and from the bow, Adele spotted a badly worn and frayed yellow rope used to keep it tied to the dock.

It was the rope that drew Adele's attention. She leaned down and inspected it more closely, comparing it to the pieces of rope in her hand. Both were colored the same, aged the same, and even smelled the same. While not a conclusive match, it was enough to give Adele pause.

She got down on her hands and knees and leaned over the dock to get a better look at the front of the little water vessel's hull. The bottom was badly damaged by repeated scrapes, evidence it had been pulled up onto and back off a beach countless times over many years.

Like that little beach on Ripple Island?

"Good morning, Adele."

Adele turned to see Tilda Ashland standing directly behind her. The hotel owner was dressed in an ankle-length light-blue summer dress and dark sandals. Her long red hair was pulled back from her lean face, making her prominent cheekbones appear even more pronounced.

"Are you looking for something?"

Adele stood up, wondering if the timing of Tilda's sudden appearance was merely coincidence or something else.

"Do you know who owns this boat?"

Tilda's eyes never left Adele. Not even for a second did she bother to look at the boat in question.

"So you are not looking for something but rather for *someone*, is that it? Might it be related to the sheriff standing outside your slip all night?"

Adele refused to be intimidated by the hard-eyed hotel owner.

"That's my business, Tilda. You said you were available to help if I needed it, remember?"

Tilda's lips pressed tightly together and widened slightly, causing deep lines to form at the corners of her mouth.

"Yes, of course."

"I also know that you watch over this resort like it was your own private kingdom. You see just about everything that happens here, don't you?"

Tilda lifted her chin upward, a gesture that was a defiant warning for Adele to remember that between them, she considered the younger woman the lesser of the two.

"Why do you wish to know who owns that boat?"

Adele's eyes wandered past Tilda to where the Roche Harbor Hotel stood. Something moved just inside one of the second-floor windows, a heavily bearded face that quickly retreated into shadow.

"I think they might wish to talk to me about something they saw."

Tilda straightened and took in a deep breath.

"Perhaps you're right, Adele. Then again, perhaps not. Will you be available later tonight?"

Adele nodded.

"Sure, what time?"

"Come to the hotel at exactly midnight. If he does in fact wish to speak with you, the front desk will escort you upstairs. If not, you will be asked to leave and this matter will be concluded. I won't have any more to say on the subject. Is that understood?"

Adele knew that despite Tilda's icy exterior, the hotel owner had just gone out of her way to help give Adele access to someone who might provide valuable information on the ongoing mystery surrounding Ripple Island and for that, she was grateful.

"I understand completely, Tilda, and thank you."

Tilda's eyes warmed for the briefest of moments.

"Don't thank me just yet. As I said, I am not certain he wishes to see you. Oh, and you never did tell me what Sheriff Pine was doing here last night."

The reporter knew Tilda, having just helped to facilitate for Adele a possible meeting with whomever was hiding inside her hotel, expected to be given an answer.

"I had dinner with Roland Soros last night, and then someone fired a gun at my car. The sheriff decided to stick around in case that someone happened to show up here looking for me."

The absurdity of the explanation was intentional, and yet Adele was amazed to see Tilda simply nod her head as if being told something as insignificant as the weather forecast.

"Roland Soros, you say? Now there's one to watch out for. As for being shot at, you're a strong woman seeking the truth. That combination will always make one a target, so please be careful. I'm just getting to know you and don't wish to see that opportunity ended by an untimely death."

It was such a dark declaration and juxtaposed with the beauty of the natural surroundings, Adele found herself having to interject some much-needed sarcasm in response to the warning.

"Yeah, I figure it's a good thing I try and stay alive a little while longer."

Tilda was genuinely amused by Adele's reply. Her laughter was surprisingly light and cheerful, like a wind chime gently pushed by a soft breeze.

"You're what my grandmother would have called a corker, Adele. I'm glad we've become acquaintances, and I look forward to one day being able to call ourselves friends. I'll see you tonight, then."

Tilda Ashland made her way back to her hotel residence, both the woman and the structure graceful and elegant extensions of Roche Harbor itself. Adele peered down at the strands of yellow rope in her hand and then looked up at the hotel wondering who at that very moment might be staring back at her.

Shortly after midnight, she hoped to find out.

12.

The Island Gazette

Human Remains Discovered Near Ripple Island
Sheriff's Office Gives First Official Statement Regarding Discovery

Local authorities discovered human remains in over one hundred feet of water just off the rocky shores of Ripple Island this past week. Rumors have run rampant since the discovery, furthered by the sheriff office's refusal to comment on what is an ongoing investigation.

This morning, the Island Gazette received the first official statement from San Juan County law enforcement regarding the gruesome discovery and will now include that statement in its entirety below.

From the office of San Juan County Sheriff Lucas Pine:

This past week, my office received an anonymous tip regarding activity near Ripple Island, an uninhabited rock approximately one nautical mile north of Roche Harbor. Upon investigation, the remains of a human body were discovered. Those remains were then sent out for forensic examination in Seattle, which revealed they were from a young woman likely between the ages of sixteen and twenty-four.

Given the nature of how the remains were found, this matter has been classified as an ongoing murder investigation. If anyone has further information regarding this case, please contact the San Juan County Sheriff's Office immediately. Your identity will remain confidential.

More information will be shared with the public once that information has been received and verified.

"So, what do you think?"

Both Avery and Bess gave Adele approving nods. Bess put down the rough copy of Adele's story that would be the lead feature in the soon-to-be published next edition of the paper.

"Succinct, the picture of the island you took is perfect, and we stay out of hot water with the sheriff because we did just like he asked—no mention of the crab pot. He came out and admitted it's a murder investigation. I imagine there will be some upset members on the council for that. Not exactly the kind of news you want circulating during the middle of tourist season. That said, we should also remember this is a story involving the death of a very young woman. What a horrible, horrible thing that was done to her."

The age of the victim had not been lost on Adele. She was herself of a similar age, which in turn made her all the more determined to try to find out who was responsible. She hadn't yet told Avery or Bess about her dinner with Roland Soros, or the gunshot that followed. She had decided to keep quiet and wait until she heard back from the sheriff on his meeting with Roland.

Bess elbowed Avery, whose eyes then widened.

"Oh! I almost forgot. Here you go, Adele. Your first byline in the paper, and now your first paycheck!"

Avery handed Adele a check made out to her in the amount of three hundred and seventeen dollars. He quickly attempted to apologize for the amount.

"I know it isn't much, but think of it as just the start of—"

Adele cut him off with a smile.

"It's just fine, thank you."

It was at that very moment her phone rang. Roland was calling her.

"I have to take this."

Bess and Avery watched Adele step outside holding her phone to her ear.

As she closed the door behind her, Adele could hear Bess telling her husband they needed to pay her more or they would lose her, a concern Avery answered by stating that for some people money wasn't the end-all, and he was certain Adele was one such person.

"Hello, Adele."

Adele paused. Roland's tone was devoid of warmth.

"I take it the sheriff spoke with you already?"

It was Roland's turn to pause.

"Yes. Why didn't you call me last night? You actually thought someone fired a gun at you? Someone I would be involved with?"

"I saw you speaking to him, Roland—the man in the hoodie. I also saw him holding what looked like a gun and running after my car. I heard you call him Sergei."

Adele detected a rustling sound, as if Roland had placed a hand over his phone.

Is he talking with someone else?

"That's ridiculous. We had a wonderful meal, good conversation, and, yes, after our dinner I was speaking with an acquaintance, but I assure you he wasn't there to do you harm, and he sure as hell didn't fire a gun at anyone."

"Is that what you told the sheriff? If you did, I'm pretty sure it's a lie. I know what I saw, Roland. Just like I know there's a bullet hole in the back of my car."

Roland unleashed a long sigh.

"Please, Adele, I don't wish to argue. You know what you think you know, and I know what I know. If someone actually shot at your car, I suggest we both try and find out who it is. Perhaps it's related to something you wrote? It wouldn't be the first time a reporter made enemies, right? Or maybe a jealous boyfriend? You know anyone around here who carries a gun?"

Adele looked down toward the ferry terminal parking lot and watched as Sheriff Pine's SUV slowly drove by.

"Are you making an accusation against someone, Roland?"

"Call it what you want, Adele. I'm just saying that everyone has a history, including a certain local sheriff."

"So what is *your* history, Mr. Soros?"

Roland chuckled.

"Back to calling me Mr. Soros, are you? Look, I like you, Adele. I don't know you well enough just yet to say how much, but I hope you give us both a chance to find out. That said, it seems clear I'm not the only one around here who has taken an interest in getting to know you better."

"How about you start by telling me who Sergei is?"

Roland's icy tone returned colder than ever.

"I see you are in no mood to talk reasonably, *Ms. Plank*. You have a good day."

Roland hung up.

Adele stared out at the greenish waters of Friday Harbor. A multitude of boats made their way into and out of the marina, while in the distance the hulking white outline of another arriving ferry dominated the landscape.

He was lying, and a person lies when they feel threatened. So why is someone with Roland Soros's means and influence feeling threatened?

And then a more troubling thought visited Adele, one that Roland Soros clearly attempted to suggest might be related to who actually fired a gun at her car. She recalled what the sheriff had said upon examining the bullet hole at the back of her MINI.

*Given your description of how close he was to the back of your car, the man is either a very bad shot **or this was meant as some kind of warning.***

"Adele, is everything OK?"

Bess had opened the office door just as Adele put her phone away.

"Yeah, everything is fine. So, the new issue comes out tomorrow?"

Bess nodded.

"Yes, right on schedule. News of the body they found is spreading throughout the islands, and now that the sheriff is officially calling it a murder investigation, interest in the story is going to increase even more. Suze told us there's even talk of a special council meeting to specifically address the case."

Adele realized she should have paid Suzanne Blatt a visit earlier. The bookstore owner was a wealth of knowledge, a seeming conduit for all things San Juan Islands–related and thus a potentially valuable resource for helpful information.

"Call me if you need anything more from me, Bess. I'll be around Friday Harbor for most the day before returning to Roche."

Initially, Adele was going to drive the short distance to the bookstore but then decided the slightly uphill walk would help clear her mind and give her a much needed, albeit brief, little workout.

The town's streets were already teeming with traffic, and there was yet more to come by afternoon. People with cameras stopped to take photos, while regular residents patiently moved past the tourists, who represented the dollars so essential to the island community's long-term economic survival. By the time she reached the bookstore, Adele had developed a thin layer of sweat across her forehead.

She saw Suze's face just inside one of the front entrance glass windows. Suze did a double-take and then gave Adele a big, welcoming smile and motioned for her to come inside. Several customers milled about within the bookstore.

"Hello there, young lady! Looking for something to read?"

Adele kept her voice low as she shook her head.

"No, I was hoping to ask you some questions, Suze. That is, if you have a little time."

Suze appeared stunned at the thought of not giving Adele whatever time she needed from her.

"Of course I have time for you! Are you kidding? You see all these people here? My business has *doubled* since you did that article of yours last year about Mr. and Mrs. Stone! I owe you a lot more than time, Adele Plank! A lot more! Go have a seat in the back, let me finish up with these customers, and then I'll make us a fresh pot of coffee, OK?"

Adele ventured to the back kitchen area and found it just as she remembered right down to the little square table and mismatched, hand-painted wooden chairs. It took nearly fifteen minutes before Suze was able to join Adele.

"I never would have imagined in this day and age I would see so many people still wanting to read books! Thank goodness for that! Let me get this coffee going, and then we'll have ourselves a good old-fashioned talk."

Soon the old Mr. Coffee that resided upon the counter next to the table was gurgling away as Suze sat down in a chair opposite Adele's.

"So, what are these questions you seem to think I might have answers to?"

Adele folded her hands in front of her and cleared her throat. She knew she likely looked as nervous as she felt.

"It's about a couple members of the community."

Suze pursed her lips together as she fought to keep from smiling.

"I see. And would these be two *men* you have questions about?"

Adele nodded.

"Yes, Lucas Pine and Roland Soros."

Suze held up a hand.

"Hold on. If we're going to discuss boys, we definitely need some coffee to keep that conversation company."

The bookstore owner stood up and poured two cups of freshly brewed coffee. She placed one in front of Adele and one in front of her own seat and then added a small pitcher of cream and a plate of sugar cubes, which she placed in the center of the table. Suze rubbed her hands together and smiled as she sat back down.

"There, that's better. All right, let's talk. Who should we start with?"

Adele took a brief sip of coffee while she considered the choice.

"Lucas Pine. What do you know about him?"

Suze's eyes narrowed.

"Hmmm, well, he was the local golden boy, high school football star, the son of a doctor who went on to serve his country in the military, but I'm guessing you want to know more than what is already common knowledge, am I right?"

"Yes, if you don't mind sharing."

Suze set her coffee cup down.

"This isn't for a story, is it? I adore Lucas's family and don't wish to see a private talk be used for public consumption. His father was my family's doctor for years, and his mother was nothing less than a wonderful, wonderful woman."

Adele shook her head.

"No, this has nothing to do with the newspaper. It's, uh, personal."

Suze smiled.

"I didn't want to presume, but I thought as much. OK, then, it's just us two girls talking about boys. Well, the only thing I can think of that some might not already know about Lucas Pine are the old rumors of some kind of trouble he got into right before he left for the army. He was back staying with his folks like he did every summer, and if I remember right, there was apparently a dispute of some kind at the Pine home that involved the police. It was winter, the slow season, when the population around here is about half that of the summer months. I recall people asking about what had happened at the Pine house. I heard a few different things, but nobody seemed to know for sure, and then all the talk just sort of went away."

Adele leaned forward in her chair, waiting for Suze to say more.

"One story was that Lucas was pulled over for driving drunk and that he resisted arrest. Another said he had a fight with his father over going into the military. And the story that was most troubling of all had to do with him beating up his girlfriend at the time because she had been caught cheating with another boy. Lucas had dated her all through high school, and it was well known they were pretty possessive of each other. Most of us figured they'd be getting married, but then Lucas went into the military, and as far as I know that was the end of the relationship."

"Do you believe any of those rumors?"

Suze added a touch of cream to her coffee.

"I don't know. What I *do* know is that based on everything I've actually seen with my own eyes, Lucas Pine is a good man. That doesn't mean he isn't capable of making a mistake or two just like we all are, but I'm happy to see him returned to these islands."

"And what about Roland Soros?"

Suze's face tightened, indicating the subject of Roland was not nearly as personally pleasing to her as that of Lucas.

"Mr. Soros is a bit more . . . complicated. I won't say I dislike him so much as I'm wary of him. About six months ago he came by here offering to buy this building from me, and apparently I'm not the only one he's been making such offers to. It seems he's always wanting to call more and more of these islands his own. I don't fault anyone for trying to grow their business, but at some point how much is too much, you know?"

"Bess said he offered to buy their building from them as well."

Suze snapped her fingers.

"See, there you go! Always trying to make himself bigger by acquiring more. Kind of rubs me the wrong way, but then again he's not all bad, either. If it weren't for him, we wouldn't have the new children's wing of our local library. He personally donated a hundred thousand dollars toward its construction. Same with the food bank. Every winter he has a thousand pounds of canned goods delivered there that I know for a fact helps to keep some of our families from going hungry. Roland Soros is a young man consumed by business, but he's also a charitable one."

A bell sounded from the front of the store, indicating another customer had arrived. Suze stood up.

"Help yourself to more coffee if you like. I'll be right back."

Adele finished her coffee as she replayed in her mind the information Suze had just given her. She kept coming back to the rumor of Lucas assaulting his girlfriend. As unlikely as it seemed, Adele knew she had to consider it a possibility.

Could that be what Roland was talking about when he suggested there was more to Lucas's history than I might wish to know?

Suze returned to her seat at the table.

"That was an interesting fella. Found him looking over my embarrassingly small Russian authors' section. Wanted to know if I had a copy of *The House of the Dead* by Dostoyevsky. Could hardly understand what he was saying because his accent was so thick." Adele's eyes widened as they peered over the brim of her coffee cup.

"Did he say his name?"

Suze took another sip of coffee.

"Yes, just his first name though—Sergei."

Adele sprung from her chair and raced toward the store entrance. By the time she was outside, Suze was calling after her.

"What is it, Adele?"

The traffic, both vehicle and pedestrian, was a slow-moving tapestry of disjointed purpose. Adele turned around and looked at a clearly concerned Suze.

"What did the man look like?"

"I'd say mid-thirties, maybe six foot or so. His head was shaved, but he had a goatee. And blue eyes. I noticed his eyes because they seemed so intense. Focused. Like he meant business. I would never have guessed him to be a reader of books, especially something so difficult to take on as Dostoyevsky."

Suze's eyes narrowed as she noted the fear and uncertainty on Adele's face.

"Should I call the police? Was that man following you?"

Adele shook her head, though she continued to look up and down the street for any sign of Sergei.

"No, I don't need the police. Though there *is* something you can do for me."

"Sure, anything I can do to help."

Twenty minutes later while driving in her car, Adele still felt a twinge of guilt for having asked Suze for the information, just as Suze no doubt felt doubly guilty for having given it. And yet, Adele wanted certain answers and knew this could be the person who might best provide them.

The source for those hoped-for answers came in the form of a name and address. She was Ophelia Norris, and she resided at 118 Cattle Point Lane.

She also happened to be Lucas Pine's former girlfriend.

13.

Cattle Point is near the southernmost region of the San Juan Islands, a place almost absent of trees and most days of the year subjected to strong winds that cut across the tall grass fields and stir up the adjacent seawater, sending it crashing into its rocky shores. The land narrows the farther south one drives until it reaches out like a defiant middle finger pointing toward neighboring Lopez Island, the two islands appearing to glare at each other across the strong, deep currents of San Juan Channel.

In the 1800s, Cattle Point was home to American soldiers stationed there as a military counterbalance to British soldiers housed some fifteen miles north along the idyllic, heavily forested shores of Garrison Bay. Both camps were constructed as a reaction to the increasing dispute between the American and British governments over who owned the islands.

By the 1870s, a treaty was signed that allowed the United States to finally lay final and permanent claim to the San Juans. The soldiers left, though some island locals continued to believe their long tenure, marked by malnutrition, disease, multiple suicides, and murders, was still carried upon the winds and rains of Cattle Point.

It was a hard, beautiful, desolate place, immersed in a natural indifference to all who visited and those few such as Ophelia Norris, who continued to make the area their home.

Ophelia's house was at the end of a long, narrow dirt road bookended by fields of tall grass that swayed against the heavy sea-infused wind, which constantly carried the whispers of the wide and often dangerous waters of the Strait of Juan de Fuca that dominated Cattle Point's southern views. The home was a decades-old single-story structure painted dark-gray with a roof that showed patches where the wind had ripped away the shingles. An older light-red jeep was parked to the right of the front door, its presence informing Adele that someone was there.

The yard, such as it was, showed more exposed dirt than grass. Two wooden planter boxes with long-dead perennials hung from the small, partially covered porch. To the left of the home was a pair of seemingly abandoned fiberglass fishing boats, the insides of which were piled high with an assortment of fishing nets and rusted-out crab and shrimp pots. To the right, a newer ten-speed bike leaned against a porch post.

Behind the home, many miles farther across both land and sea, loomed the shadowy mass of the Olympic Mountains. The only unnatural fixture upon that majestic horizon was a white lighthouse that stood still and silent half a mile to the west.

The front door of the house opened even before Adele was able to fully exit her car. She looked up to see a tall, athletically built figure with a head of thick, shoulder-length, wavy blonde hair staring back at her. The woman wore black biker shorts that further complemented her long, muscular legs. The shorts were accompanied by a gray sweatshirt that, though less form-fitting, was unable to completely conceal the generous swell of her breasts.

"Can I help you?"

The voice indicated a personality similar to the wind that pummeled the property: strong, direct, and not something to be trifled with.

"Are you Ophelia Norris?"

The woman's eyes hardened as she gave Adele an abbreviated nod.

"Yeah, who's asking?"

"Ms. Norris, my name is Adele Plank. I'm with the *Island Gazette*, but my visit here doesn't involve the newspaper."

Ophelia rose to her full height of nearly six feet while putting a hand on each of her hips.

"So, how about you tell me what this *does* involve?"

Adele cleared her throat.

"Uh, it involves Lucas Pine."

Ophelia's mouth formed a hard slash above her strong chin.

"You mean the sheriff? What does *he* want?"

Adele realized she had not thought through how the conversation with Ophelia might go prior to its rather precarious beginning. Part of her wanted to get back into her car and drive away, but the greater part of her, that inquisitive nature that demanded answers, won the internal war within and instead forged ahead.

"He didn't send me. I'm here on my own. I was hoping you could answer some questions I had about Lucas when he was younger—something that might have happened right before he left for the army."

Ophelia's head tilted sideways a few inches as she appeared to reassess what Adele's true motivations might be.

"Why in the hell would you care about my ancient history with Lucas Pine? We were both just stupid kids then. Are you dating him or something?"

There was an edge to Ophelia's tone, a hint she was not one to shrink from confrontation should someone find themselves on the wrong side of her sensibilities. Adele was quick to try to ensure her she wasn't there to do that.

"No, but I *am* getting to know him and was recently told about something that might have happened between you two that involved the police."

Ophelia appeared to relax. She rolled her eyes at Adele, dismissing her as merely an annoyance and not a threat.

"That's just stupid island rumors. I have nothing against Lucas. We dated, we broke up. That's it. He was the football star and I was the cheerleader, and then time goes on, and neither of us are those things anymore. People grow up and grow apart. That's hardly worth you driving all the way out here to talk about, don't you think?"

Ophelia's eyes narrowed as she pointed at Adele.

"Say, you look familiar. Have we spoken before?"

"No, I don't believe so."

"Hold on, I know who you are! You're the one who did the story on the writer and his wife and the old sheriff who kept her locked up all those years. Why are you slumming for the *Island Gazette*? I'd figure you'd be with some big city newspaper by now."

Adele shrugged. It was a relaxed gesture that belied the cautious vigilance she still felt was necessary around Ophelia.

"Oh, I had offers, but there's something about this place, these islands, that brought me back."

Ophelia's face took on an expression of having just smelled something particularly offensive.

"Really? Huh. Well, give it time. Sooner or later you'll be dying to get off these damn rocks."

"You live out here by yourself?"

The former high school cheerleader shrugged.

"Yeah, my parents retired to Florida. Dad was a local fisherman for more than forty years. He used to take me out with him a lot when I was a kid. All that's left of those times are memories and those two old boats rotting away in the yard. I have a brother, but he's a financial consultant in Chicago. So I guess that leaves me here holding down the fort for now. It hasn't even been ten years since graduation, but boy does high school seem like it was ages ago. Weird how life seems to pick up speed after every year that passes."

Ophelia looked out toward the water as her mouth collapsed into a pronounced frown. Adele gathered her courage and asked something she knew might result in an abrupt end to the conversation.

"If you could, would you go back? Would you like to be with Lucas again?"

Ophelia crossed her arms across her chest. The wind began to pick up, pushing Adele onto the balls of her feet.

"Part of me wants to call you a nosey bitch for asking that kind of question. I suppose that's your nature, though, isn't it? I also promise you that if a word of this ends up in that little rag newspaper you work for, I'll personally hunt you down and kick your ass."

"Like I said, I'm not here about the newspaper, Ms. Norris. I was just trying to get confirmation or denial about the rumor involving you and Lucas and the police right before Lucas left the islands for the military."

Ophelia shook her head.

"No, what you're doing here is trying to find out if Lucas can be trusted, and that's not for me to say. As for any rumors, I don't care to bring up the past, at least not that part of it."

"Did Lucas Pine assault you?"

Ophelia's mouth fell open and her eyes simmered with shocked outrage.

"What? Lucas? No, he did no such thing! Is that what someone told you? That he *hurt* me? Lucas would never do that. *Never.*"

Ophelia stepped off her porch, which caused Adele to subconsciously move backward until she was pressed against the bumper of her MINI.

"Who told you that? Who put that idea into your head?"

Given her angry defense of Lucas's character, it became clear to Adele that Ophelia was not nearly as detached from her past relationship with him as she would have others believe.

Ophelia stopped and lowered her gaze to the hard-packed dirt at her feet. Her eyes repeatedly darted to the left and right as if trying to remember something, and then her head lifted, and she spit out a single word at Adele.

"Roland."

Adele said nothing, her silence giving Ophelia confirmation she had correctly guessed the source of the accusation against Lucas.

"That, spoiled, sniveling, little brat! Some people never change."

Adele pushed aside her lingering, troubled silence.

"What do you mean some people never change? Was Roland involved in whatever happened between you and Lucas all those years ago?"

Ophelia's mouth opened and then abruptly shut. She glared at Adele with fists tightly clenched at her side.

"Are you working for *him*? Are you one of Roland's stooges? Is that why you're really here? You tell that son of a bitch to go to hell! My family won't sell! Not to see a damn casino and parking lot take this property's place."

Adele had no idea what Ophelia was raging on about, but she paid very close attention, knowing it might later prove important.

"It's time for you to leave, and don't come back. I have nothing to say to the likes of you."

"Ms. Norris, I assure you, I'm not here on behalf of anyone but myself. I don't know what your history is with Mr. Soros, but it doesn't involve me."

Ophelia took a slow, deliberate step toward Adele. Her jaw was clenched so tight her mouth could barely move when she spoke.

"Lady, I asked nice. You better get moving now or I might end up doing something *you'll* regret."

Adele didn't wish to see if Ophelia was willing to make good on her promise of potential violence. Instead, she made a hasty retreat into her car and drove away. When she glanced into the rearview mirror, she saw Ophelia standing in front of her home, intently watching her departure.

Early evening was upon the islands, and Adele's midnight meeting with Tilda Ashland in Roche Harbor awaited.

14.

"You sure seem to have a knack for making my life more difficult, I'll give you that."

Adele stared through the windshield of her MINI while also trying to maintain her composure as the sheriff stood outside the car window she had just rolled down at his request. He had pulled her over a mile from the Roche Harbor entrance and walked up with eyes flashing almost as much as the blue lights atop his SUV.

Tall evergreen trees crowded both sides of the road, nearly blocking out the sun and bathing the area in shadow.

"Are you going to just ignore me, now? What the hell would make you drive out to Ophelia's place, anyways? Asking if I *assaulted* her? Was it really Roland who put that damn idea into your head?"

Adele felt her own anger rising within her. She finally locked eyes with Lucas and didn't look away.

"It wasn't Roland's doing, not entirely. I like to know the truth, is all."

Adele paused, uncertain if she should proceed with questioning the already upset sheriff, and then pushed caution aside and did just that.

"Well, did you or didn't you do something to Ophelia that required the police to question you?"

Lucas cursed softly as he turned away from the car. When he turned back around, his face betrayed the hurt and confusion the accusation evoked in him.

"Look, there *was* an incident at my house years ago, but that's a private matter. I need you to respect that, OK? And please, whatever you do, don't go bothering Ophelia with those kinds of questions."

"Why not, Lucas? What are you hiding?"

The sheriff grimaced.

"Ms. Plank, please, I am asking as nice as I know how that you not go around stirring things up like this. My job is literally on the line here."

Adele gripped the steering wheel tightly.

"I recall you asked me for help, Sheriff. Remember?"

Lucas shook his head.

"I asked that you let me know if you came across any information that might help with the case of the remains we found out by Ripple Island. I didn't say *anything* about you showing up unannounced at the house of a former girlfriend from high school and asking her if I assaulted her. C'mon, Adele, you were out of line and you know it."

Doubt and guilt began to work their way into Adele's mind.

Maybe he's right. Maybe I went too far.

"I don't want us to be enemies, Adele, far from it. That said, I don't like getting phone calls from a woman screaming at me because of something you did without thinking it through. I know you have something in you that seems to push you to find the truth, but you gotta remember you're dealing with human beings here, people with their own lives, their own problems . . . their own secrets."

Adele sighed but didn't speak. She didn't know what to say, not yet convinced she was actually in the wrong for having talked to Ophelia Norris.

"So, was it Roland who put you up to that visit out to Ophelia's place? And if it was, don't you think he might have his own personal motivation for doing so?"

Adele glanced up at the sheriff and then looked away.

"I don't want to be the cause of problems between you and Roland, Lucas."

The sheriff rested his arms over the MINI's door frame so that his face was at the same level as Adele's. He attempted a reassuring smile, though his eyes still hinted at the anger and disappointment he felt toward Adele for her recently concluded journey out to Cattle Point.

"I'd say it's a little late for that, Ms. Plank. Clearly Roland Soros has taken an interest in you."

Lucas stood back up and looked down the road as a light-blue four-door sedan approached from the opposite lane and then drove past them, likely on its way to Friday Harbor.

"And I suppose it's no secret that's one thing me and Roland currently have in common."

An awkward, uncomfortable silence took the place of the anger that had dominated the roadside conversation between Lucas and Adele. The sheriff coughed into his hand and then pretended to adjust the belt that held his gun in place on his right hip.

"So, where you off to?"

"On my way home to Roche. That is, until some asshole sheriff decided to pull me over."

Lucas laughed.

Adele enjoyed the sound, but also knew their relationship, whatever it was or might one day be, would continue to prove a complicated one.

"Yeah, I guess I deserve that. You know, my dad asked about you."

"Really? Why?"

Two more cars drove by. They saw the sheriff's SUV lights flashing, slowed down, and then once confident he wouldn't pull them over, they picked up speed and vanished around the curve in the two-lane road.

"He wanted you to come along with us on Sunday to visit my mother's grave. We go out there once a month to leave flowers. It's a short walk from the resort. There's a graveyard out there, and the mausoleum. You've never been?"

Adele shook her head. She had read the visitor pamphlets and seen the signs indicating its presence but had yet to journey out to the trail east of the Roche Harbor resort that led to the famous burial grounds that contained graves from as far back as the 1800s, when the property was a valuable limestone quarry owned by nineteenth-century Pacific Northwest business magnate John S. McMillin.

"We'll be by around nine. You're welcome to join us. We could meet you in front of the hotel. It's about a twenty-minute walk from there."

"Uh, yeah, sure, why not? If you really think it's OK. I don't want to intrude."

Lucas tapped the top of the MINI with the palm of his hand.

"We'll see you tomorrow. Until then, drive safe."

Adele watched the sheriff get back into his SUV, turn off the lights, make a U-turn, and then drive south toward Friday Harbor, leaving her alone still parked on the side of the road.

He pulls me over, we yell at each other, and then I agree to meet him on Sunday to visit his mother's grave? What the heck am I doing?

Adele had no answer to the hot-and-cold nature of her burgeoning relationship with Lucas Pine. She was about to start her car and pull it back onto the road when her phone rang. It was Roland.

"Just checking in, Adele, and wondering if perhaps you might agree to join me for dinner later this evening? I know our last conversation ended badly, and I wish to both apologize and attempt to make up for that."

Adele made certain not to mention her trip to Ophelia Norris's home or the argument with Lucas that followed.

"I'm sorry, Roland, I'm busy tonight."

"Oh, is it newspaper business or personal?"

Adele looked up to see a black pickup truck with darkly tinted windows slowly driving in the opposite lane toward her parked car. It appeared to be doing no more than ten miles an hour. And then it stopped altogether on the side of the road directly across from the parked MINI. The truck's engine revved loudly several times. Adele's eyes strained to see through the window tint to get a look at the driver.

Shaved head. Goatee.

It was the man she had seen in the parking lot pushing Roland against his Mercedes after the dinner at the Gooseberry Inn. The same man likely responsible for the bullet hole in the back of her car, and the one who just a couple of hours earlier had followed her into the bookstore.

Sergei.

"Adele, are you still there?"

"That man I saw you with in the parking lot, the one named Sergei, he's been following me, Roland. He's sitting inside his truck staring at me right now. Did you put him up to this? Are you trying to scare me? Why would you do that?"

After a slight pause, Roland answered in a tone that suggested newly arrived concern.

"If in fact Sergei has been following you, I promise I have nothing to do with it. Where are you?"

"I'm in my car on the side of the road about a mile from Roche."

The truck revved its engine once again.

"What are you doing on the side of the road? Are you having car trouble?"

Before Adele could answer, she saw the truck's driver door begin to open. She placed her phone on the MINI's passenger seat and waited as Sergei emerged fully from the truck. He was dressed in a red T-shirt and blue jeans. There was neither darkness nor hoodie to hide his face. His shaved scalp, dark eyes, and downturned mouth lent him an undeniably sinister presence.

Though gripped by trepidation, Adele decided then, sinister or not, she wasn't going to so easily give Sergei what he wanted from her, namely her fear of him.

The Russian's eyes widened as she was next to open her own car door and step outside, where she proceeded to stare back at him.

"What do you want, Sergei? You going to shoot up my car again?"

Sergei smirked as he shook his head. His accent was thick, the voice a low growl.

"I didn't shoot at you. If I did, you'd already be dead."

"I asked what you want. Why are you following me?"

The Russian shrugged, the smirk softening almost to a smile.

"I am just making introduction. And perhaps then you will decide it is not always best to ask so many questions, yes? Perhaps you will know it is best to keep your mouth shut."

"So you *are* trying to scare me. You should know that only makes me want to find out the reasons why you would want me to keep quiet."

Sergei folded his muscular arms across his chest. Each forearm was covered in elaborate multicolored tattoos.

"Ah, when you say such things, it is *you* who now tries to intimidate *me*!"

"I'm just doing my job, Sergei. You're not the first man who has tried to shut me up."

The smirk returned.

"It is as I said. If I wanted you dead, you would be. I'm here to make certain that doesn't become only option left."

"Yeah, so I don't end up with my body stuffed into a crab pot and sent to the bottom of the sea?"

Sergei frowned.

"What?"

Adele watched the Russian's face closely, trying to determine if his confusion was genuine or fabricated but found the results inconclusive.

Both their heads turned at the sound of a roaring motor that indicated a vehicle approaching at high speed. A black Mercedes came to a screeching halt directly in front of Sergei's truck. Roland exited his car and pointed at the Russian, screaming at him as he did so.

"Get your ass out of here! I told you, she is off limits!"

Sergei's eyes flared. He took several steps toward Roland while snarling his rebuke.

"You don't threaten *me*, Roland! I threaten *you*!"

Roland's anger did not diminish in the face of the glowering Russian.

"Not around here, you don't. This isn't Vancouver. This is *my* home, *my* people, *my* rules. And she is *my* friend. You hurt her, and I will end you, understood?"

Adele watched as Sergei's fists clenched. It was clear he was about to strike Roland.

The blast of a car horn sounded to her left. A green station wagon with a family of six waited for Roland and Sergei to get out of the road. The Russian looked at the wagon and then at Adele. Whatever punishment he wished to deliver on both Roland and Adele would have to wait—for now. He took a deep breath and stared back at the island businessman.

"This is not over, Roland. You and me, we are going to have serious discussion very soon. I won't risk everything because you want that little piece of ass standing over there."

The Russian turned around, walked back to his truck, and sped off, followed by the station wagon's much slower departure. Roland crossed the road and looked down at Adele.

"I'm so sorry. I was only a few miles away, and when you stopped talking on the phone, I drove as fast as I could to get here. I would *never* let Sergei harm you. I hope you believe me when I tell you that."

"Who the hell is he to you, Roland? What exactly are you involved with? I'm pretty sure that man just threatened to kill me!"

Roland's hand ran over tightly shut eyes.

"His bark is a lot worse than his bite, I promise."

"*What?* What does that even mean?"

Roland bit down on his lower lip as he shook his head.

"At this point, I'm not even sure I know. Someday I might explain all of this to you, but for now I just can't do that."

Roland turned around and let out an exhausted sigh.

"The vision I have for these islands, the work and the risks involved, it requires certain complications. Sergei happens to be one of those complications."

Adele reached out and placed her hands onto Roland's shoulders and gently turned him around so he was again facing her.

"That man isn't just a complication. He's dangerous."

Roland looked into Adele's eyes. There was no hint of his wealth, his privilege, or his determination to acquire even more money and influence. He was just a man who found himself starting to care for a young woman who had just recently entered his life.

"He won't bother you again. Give me a chance to prove to you that I'm the better man."

Though he hadn't spoken his name, it was clear Roland had just defined Adele's choices for her. She was to choose him or Lucas. That didn't sit well with her. Adele pushed herself away and let her disappointment be known with a shake of her head.

"You don't get to tell me what my own options are, Roland. Your attempt to do just that indicates you're as arrogant and self-absorbed as some people around here seem to think you are. I'm going home. All I ask is that you keep that Russian stooge of yours attached to whatever leash you think you have him on, understood?"

Roland's face fell into itself. He was clearly saddened by Adele's forceful rebuke.

"I didn't mean to make you feel as if you had to make a choice. I'm sorry."

Roland turned and was halfway to his car when he stopped to look back at Adele as she prepared to get into her MINI.

"Will you be telling the sheriff about Sergei threatening you?"

Adele held up both hands as she shrugged.

"Yeah, that seems like a no-brainer, don't you think?"

Roland stood motionless next to the Mercedes, waging an internal battle over what to say next. When he finally spoke, it was with but a single word, though Adele took it to hold a multitude of potential meanings.

"OK."

For the second time that day, Adele was left alone on the side of the road. Only this time she had no intention of waiting around to see who might show up next.

15.

Phillip Ozere, Tilda's long-serving and devoted hotel manager, was just as Adele remembered him: tall, dressed in a white dress shirt and black slacks, and largely indifferent to Adele's presence inside the hotel.

"Welcome back, Ms. Plank. Please have a seat next to the fireplace, and I'll let you know if Ms. Ashland is available to greet you."

It was midnight at Roche Harbor. The hotel guests were safely locked away behind the doors of their rooms. The lobby, much like the resort and marina facilities outside, was still and silent, a thing in slumber, resting for the day to come.

"Ms. Plank, please follow me."

Adele rose from her chair next to the stone-hearth fireplace and made her way to the wood-framed stairs behind the lobby's large oak check-in desk. He led her to the hotel's third-floor hallway and then pointed to the very end of the corridor, where Tilda's shadowy form nodded her approval.

Without saying anything more, Phillip returned downstairs, leaving Adele standing alone at one end of the hall looking back at the still-waiting Tilda Ashland.

Each step Adele took upon the wood floor created a dull thump, like that of a large grandfather clock as it counted off the seconds. She passed several guest room doors both to her left and to her right. By the time she reached the hotel owner, Adele's eyes had fully adjusted to the gloom.

Tilda looked down at Adele and gave the younger woman a thin smile. It was a gesture meant to reassure Adele, but it did little more than cause her to take a slow, hard swallow. Tilda Ashland was intimidating enough in the full light of day. When accompanied by near darkness, her presence was even more unnerving.

"Hello, Adele."

Adele nodded and then pointed at the last door on the right, in front of which Tilda appeared to be standing guard.

"Is the owner of the boat I asked you about in there?"

Tilda's carefully executed thin smile vanished, replaced by the hard lines and simmering eyes far more common to her visage. Her voice, though a hushed whisper, somehow filled Adele's ears like far-off thunder that warned of an approaching storm.

"This hotel has long been a place for some to hide from the prying eyes and mewling cries of a world drowning in its own insignificance. The man behind this door deserves to have his wish for anonymity respected and maintained, as do *all* my guests. Is that understood?"

Adele was fascinated by Tilda's cloaked-in-secrecy introduction to the apparent owner of the ragged skiff from which she had matched the remnants of rope recently taken from Ripple Island.

"I'm a reporter. Protecting a source's identity is part of my job. I give you my word, Tilda. If this person doesn't wish for his identity to be known, I'll do nothing to endanger that."

The smile returned, absent any suggestion of warmth as Tilda's shadow appeared to fill the entirety of the hallway.

"I have promised my guest that very thing, Adele. Don't you dare make a liar of me."

"I don't intend to, Tilda. The fact is you scare the hell out of me."

This time Tilda's smile was genuine, joined by a mischievous twinkle in her eyes.

"I know."

Tilda reached down and slowly opened the door into the small guest room that was across the hall from her own private residence. The small space smelled of sweat and seawater. Light from a television shot out into the hallway, momentarily blinding Adele. After blinking several times, she looked inside and found a man seated in a dark-colored upholstered chair facing a TV with his back to her. His right hand lifted upward slowly while making a come-here motion, directing her to step inside.

Tilda gently pushed the back of Adele's shoulders and then closed the door, leaving Adele alone with the stranger. His hand reached out behind him to point at the right side of the room.

"Please take a seat on the corner of the bed, there."

Adele did as she was asked. The narrow bed was neatly made, its red cover pulled tight around the corners of the mattress. A single backpack lay underneath the room's only window, which looked out onto the narrow paved road that ran along the back portion of the hotel property. A copy of the most recent issue of the *Island Gazette* lay on the night table adjacent to the left side of the bed. The white painted six-panel door to the bathroom on the right side of the bed was closed.

The man continued to stare at the silent images playing across the television screen. Eventually, Adele began to do the same. It was then she realized it was a movie from her childhood, a summer blockbuster action-romance film released fourteen years ago.

"If I were to tell you one secret, will you promise to keep another?"

Adele leaned forward on the bed.

"I'm sorry, what did you say?"

The man's hands gripped the tops of the armrests of the chair he sat in. He repeated the question.

"I said, if I were to tell you one secret, will you promise to keep another?"

The man spoke in soft, gentle tones but with unusually clear and concise diction. Each syllable and vowel was formed and delivered with near-perfect articulation. Adele leaned to her right, trying to spy a glimpse of his face. She could see a bit of silver hair peeking out from the side of the high-backed chair.

"Yes, yes I would."

"Do you know who I once was?"

The odd past tense wording of the question caused Adele to squint. She remained on guard, wondering what the stranger was up to.

"I think you might be the guy who asked me about my friend's runabout the other day. I'm also pretty sure you've been watching me from the hotel since then."

The man shifted in the chair.

"Your friend is the writer, correct?"

"Yes, Decklan Stone."

The walls of the small room seemed to expand slightly, as if even the hotel itself were eagerly anticipating what might be said next.

"I don't wish to be a part of the investigation, Ms. Plank. Do you understand?"

"What investigation?"

The man growled his annoyance.

"The one involving the remains of the young woman that were found, of course."

Adele's eyes flew open.

"You're the anonymous tip the sheriff spoke of!"

The man's hands folded onto his lap.

"That is correct."

Adele looked down to see her own hands tightly gripping the end of the bed.

"Why are you telling me this? Why not talk to the sheriff about what you know?"

"Because if I do that, I won't be able to have my new life back. Instead, I'll be forced to return to my old one. I can't do that. I *won't* do that."

Adele felt the first stirrings of frustration. She wanted him to share what he knew, but instead he continued to communicate in half riddles.

"A young woman died. If you have any information that might help the authorities find out who was responsible, you have an obligation to get that information to them."

"And that is why I invited you here. You are on good terms with the new sheriff, yes?"

Adele turned her head toward the sound of one of the guest doors opening and closing from somewhere in the hallway outside the room.

"Yeah, I suppose so. Why?"

"I don't necessarily have anything to tell you that I didn't already tell the sheriff's office when I left instructions on where they would find the body."

"But he'll want to interview you."

The stranger nodded.

"*Exactly*, and that's where you come in. I wish to do the right thing. I want the person responsible for dumping that body to be made accountable. What I won't give up is my continued future as a dead man. So let me tell you what I know, and let the same observant mind of yours that allowed you to so quickly solve the case of your writer friend and his missing wife do the same regarding the mystery of the remains that were dumped into the waters of Ripple Island."

"Did you actually see the body being dropped into the water?"

The man almost turned around to face Adele but then stopped just short of doing so.

"I saw enough to know it was a crab pot that was used to hold the remains."

Adele stiffened. The sheriff had not yet shared that piece of information with the public.

"How many were on the boat?"

"I saw just one. I couldn't tell if the person was male or female. The face was covered by some kind of hat or hood. I watched them stuff pieces of something into the crab trap, and then in the light, it was a full moon, I saw a severed human head. I saw the eyes, the long hair and knew it had been a woman. The head was the last thing to be put into the pot before it was thrown overboard. There was no rope or buoy attached to it, which told me the contents inside were not meant to be found. And then as quietly as it had arrived, the boat was gone, leaving no sign it had been there at all."

Adele recalled her visit to Ripple Island and the unusually loud speedboat that had approached the island and then sped away.

"It wasn't a loud boat with side hull exhaust and a dark-blue hull that you saw that night?"

"No, I'm quite certain it was an all-white hull with an outboard on the back that hardly made any noise, the same as a thousand other boats moving about these islands."

"And you were on Ripple Island in the middle of the night when this took place?"

The stranger's heavily bearded face turned toward the bed just enough that Adele was able to see his dark eyes glance at her.

"Yes."

"Why? That island is little more than a big rock. How did you happen to be there at that particular moment?"

The man leaned forward in his chair and hit the pause button on the VCR housed directly beneath the television. The lean, handsome face of the movie's leading man filled the screen.

"That rock, as you call it, is my home."

Adele recalled the smooth bark of the shrub she and Avery had used to tie up to the beach during their recent visit to the island, and her certainty that it indicated someone had been tying up to that same bush for some time.

"You mean to say you visit the island, right? You don't actually *live* there."

The stranger shook his head.

"I meant *exactly* what I said, but that is not the purpose of this conversation. I am here to tell you what I saw that night, and that is *all* I intend to speak to you about. I want this case solved. I want you to help the sheriff to solve it, because only then will I be able to return to the place I intend to live out the remainder of my days."

Adele had to consider the possibility the man was beyond merely eccentric—that he might actually be delusional. And yet there was the matter of his knowledge of the young woman's remains being placed into a crab pot.

"Was the boat you saw that night older or newer?"

The man shrugged.

"I'm not sure. It was no more than twenty feet long. The helm was on the right side with an open fishing area in the back. Oh, there is something I just remembered. The anchor light, the one you normally see sitting up two or three feet on the stern, was broken off, as if something had hit it."

"You didn't include that information in the message you left with the sheriff's office?"

"No, as I told you, I just remembered."

"And that's it? That's everything you saw that night?"

A vehicle's headlights splashed across the single window, briefly bathing the hotel room in a halogen glow. Only after the light dissipated was Adele given her answer.

"Yes, that is all I know."

Adele stood up from the bed and moved toward the door as the man remained seated and unmoving with his back to her while staring at the face still frozen in place on the TV.

"If I have any more questions, will I still be able to contact you here?"

The man reached out in front of him and pressed the VCR's play button. The film resumed, an apparent signal to Adele that their conversation was over. As Adele began to open the door to leave, the stranger offered up a final comment.

"Good luck to you, Ms. Plank. I do hope you find the one who murdered that poor girl. They're out there somewhere. And if they've killed already, it seems quite possible they would be willing to do so again, don't you think?"

Adele stepped out into the hallway and closed the door behind her. She felt Tilda's gaze even before turning her head and discovering the hotel owner standing at the opposite end of the hall, dressed in a floor-length black robe, her long hair spread out across her shoulders, a more substantial extension of the darkness that enveloped her.

Cripes! It's like she goes out of her way to creep me out.

Tilda waited for Adele to make the short trip down the hall and then led her back to the empty lobby below. It appeared even Phillip had finally left for the night. Tilda looked Adele up and down before clasping her hands behind her back.

"I will remind you yet again of your promise to respect the privacy of my guests."

Adele was tired and feeling less inclined to pretend to dance to Tilda Ashland's self-important tune. She just wanted to get some sleep.

"I really don't care who that man upstairs *thinks* he is, Tilda." The hotel owner appeared momentarily amused by Adele's dismissive retort.

"I trust the information he provided will be of some use?"

"I hope so, but it's too early to say. Now if you don't mind, I need to go to bed."

Tilda's brows arched.

"Something requires you to be up early?"

Adele grunted.

"You know, for someone who is always demanding privacy for their guests, you sure are nosy about everyone else's business around here."

Tilda flinched. She wasn't accustomed to someone speaking to her as Adele did, and certainly not inside her own hotel. Her response was to deliver an especially pronounced scowl, but having already seen it so many times before, its power over Adele was greatly diminished.

"I'm not being rude, Tilda, just tired."

Adele stepped outside and took a deep breath, trying to clear her head. She looked behind her, fully expecting to see Tilda watching her departure from the other side of a hotel window with the all too familiar scowl still firmly affixed to her face. Tilda wasn't there. The lobby was again empty. And tomorrow would begin with a visit to a cemetery.

16.

Edmund Pine really did remember her. He may not have been able to recall Adele's name, but his wide eyes and even wider smile made clear he knew her face as he welcomed her with a firm hug just outside the entrance to Tilda Ashland's Roche Harbor Hotel.

"Hello there, young lady! Lucas said you'd be joining us on our walk. Thank you so much for being here."

Adele felt the retired doctor's hands squeezing her own as he gave his son an approving nod. He was dressed in a light-brown suit, white dress shirt, and navy blue tie, all of which was matched with a dark-gray wool hat.

"She's a nice girl, Lucas. And I doubt I'm the only one around here noticing."

Lucas Pine was not in uniform, instead wearing a pair of form-fitting jeans, white T-shirt, and denim jacket that Adele gave her own enthusiastic, albeit unspoken, approval.

"I know, Dad."

"Well, then, perhaps you might need to up your game, son!"

Edmund's cheerful morning disposition was infectious. Both Adele and Lucas chuckled at the old man's desire to see them get to know each other better.

It was just after nine in the morning. Low-hanging white clouds covered the entirety of the resort. The air hinted at the promise of rain to come later that day. Lucas extended his hand to the left, toward a narrow paved road that disappeared into a thick forest of pine and red-barked madrone trees.

Dr. Pine rubbed his hands together.

"OK, then, let's get a move on. You know how Mother hates it when people are late."

The doctor, despite his age, appeared to have little difficulty making the nearly half-mile journey to the cemetery hidden within the Roche Harbor woods that bordered the resort property.

"He's in great shape, isn't he?"

Lucas, who was walking next to Adele, looked up to where his father strode some forty yards in front of them.

"Yeah, that's what makes it even more tragic. His physical health is fine, but his mind is failing him. A specialist told me a few months back that he might live another ten years or more—but he most likely won't remember any of it."

"But he remembers the way to your mom's grave?"

Lucas shrugged.

"I know, right? Like I said before, the mornings are always best for him. Then as the day goes on, he gets tired, even cranky sometimes, and by evening, he really starts to struggle."

Edmund stopped and pointed at a clearing in the woods.

"Right over there! Three of them!"

Adele and Lucas looked to where the doctor indicated and saw a mother deer and two white-speckled fawns nibbling on a cluster of flowering plants. They stood watching the deer eat for several minutes before the doctor continued walking farther on up the road as he motioned for the other two to follow.

"Mom loved this place. She said it was one of the most sacred places in all of the islands."

Adele was quick to understand how one could come to arrive at that opinion. The road led to an even narrower dirt path marked by a small hand-carved wooden arrow with the white-lettered word *cemetery* painted on it. Leading farther into the woods, the path was sometimes broken apart by the myriad tree roots that dissected the earth. The surroundings had a unique mix of natural forested solitude and human remembrance, something intangible that was felt more than merely seen.

Dr. Pine, with his hands stuffed into the front pockets of his slacks, whistled a happy tune to himself as he nimbly made his way deeper and deeper into the island forest.

Soon Adele spotted her first grave, a weathered off-white tombstone engraved with the date of 1922 that was nearly overgrown by green-leaf vines. She saw another grave and yet another, until the woods around her were dotted with burial markers. The pine-scented air was both cool and still, and from somewhere to the south, Adele thought she heard the groan of distant thunder.

Lucas pointed to a white tombstone, in front of which his father already stood, holding his hat in his hands.

"There she is."

The name on the grave marker read Katarina Pine.

The doctor leaned down and brushed away some dry leaves that partially covered the grave and then stood up and gave his son a teary-eyed smile.

"Come say hello to your mother, Lucas."

The sheriff stood next to his father and put his arm around his shoulders. Both men stared down at the grave for several more seconds in silence, while Adele quietly watched from underneath a tree some twenty feet away. Lucas turned to look back at her and then left his dad alone at the gravesite.

"He'll be here for a while. If you want, I can show you the mausoleum. It'll give us a chance to talk."

The mention of talking elicited a nervous tightening in Adele's stomach. She had not yet told the sheriff of the threat from Sergei, or of Roland's quick action to intervene on her behalf. And then there was her midnight meeting with the man who claimed to have been an eyewitness to the disposing of the body found near Ripple Island, a man whose existence Adele had promised not to reveal to anyone else.

So many secrets.

"You OK?"

Adele gave Lucas a quick nod, wanting to get moving again to try to take her mind off the task of keeping track of all the things she should and shouldn't say to him.

"Yeah, I'm fine."

"Dad, we're going to the mausoleum. Be back in about a half an hour."

Dr. Pine waved at Lucas and Adele and then winked.

"Good for you, son! Show her you're more than just a pretty face."

Lucas rolled his eyes.

"He can't remember what he ate for dinner yesterday, but he still remembers how to embarrass me."

Adele followed Lucas as he led her down a series of dirt paths until they reached a gravel road. Another handmade sign pointed the way toward the mausoleum.

"Are there actually people buried there?"

Lucas glanced up at the darkening sky and then nodded.

"Yeah, it's kind of creepy but beautiful at the same time. It's made out of some of the limestone they mined around here. Looks like something you'd see in ancient Rome or Greece."

Adele assumed there was at least a bit of exaggeration in the sheriff's description, but upon arriving at the mausoleum, she instead found his words didn't entirely do the structure justice.

A massive iron gate marked the entrance to the site, with a sign that read Afterglow Vista. Beyond the gate was a wide path leading to a set of equally wide stone stairs around which were five large marble pillars arranged in a circle that rose more than twenty feet above the earth. Inside the circle was a platform that housed a round limestone table around which six weathered stone chairs were arranged.

Lucas pointed to the chair nearest to where Adele stood.

"Each chair has the ashes of an original member of the McMillan family placed inside of it. They were the ones who once owned the limestone mine and all of the property that later became the Roche Harbor resort."

Adele's eyes widened as she looked from one chair to the next.

"So each of these chairs is a grave?"

"Yeah, that's right. And do you notice the space where it looks like a chair is missing?"

Adele nodded and then waited for the explanation, fascinated by the story behind the Roche Harbor mausoleum.

"That space represents one of patriarch John McMillan's sons, who he had a falling out with. The son left Roche Harbor never to return, and that's why the space was left empty without a chair."

Adele wasn't aware she was staring at Lucas with a faint smile on her face until he cleared his throat.

"Uh, am I boring you, Ms. Plank?"

"No, just the opposite. It seems your dad is right. You *are* more than just a pretty face. You could pass for downright scholarly, Sheriff Pine. A book in one hand and a gun in the other."

Adele took a few quick photos of the mausoleum with her phone, while Lucas waited for her at the bottom of the steps. He looked up at her and proceeded to take out his own phone as well.

"You mind if I take your picture?"

Adele winced, conscious that she was wearing a baggy sweatshirt and cargo shorts with a pair of mismatched socks and had her hair pulled back in a simple ponytail.

"I'm afraid I'm not looking my best."

Lucas lowered his phone.

"From where I'm standing, you look just fine."

Adele tried to pull off a natural smile, knew she failed, and then shrugged as Lucas snapped the picture. By the time she reached the bottom of the stairs, Adele had decided to share with Lucas her most recent encounter with Sergei, but before she could open her mouth, Lucas spoke first.

"I put out an APB on that Russian. My deputies, border agents, state ferry personnel, and fish and wildlife are all on the lookout based on your description. If he's around here, we'll find him."

Adele's eyes narrowed as she pursed her lips. The sheriff cocked his head to the side.

"What?"

"I saw him again yesterday—Sergei."

Lucas repeated the same question, though much more loudly.

"WHAT?"

"Yeah, it was on the side of the road. The very same place you pulled me over. He tried to scare me into not asking any more questions about him and whatever he is involved in with Roland."

Lucas placed his hands on his hips as he shook his head.

"Adele, why didn't you call me? You were out there all alone with that guy?"

"Not exactly. Roland showed up. He told Sergei to get the hell out of there, and Sergei did."

Lucas straightened to his full height.

"Oh, I see. Well that's interesting given I specifically told Roland to contact me as soon as he saw this Sergei again. That means I have *two* people who failed to let me know they saw him."

"I *was* going to tell you, Lucas. I told you just now."

"But you didn't tell me yesterday, did you? And yet you had time to drive out to Cattle Point and interrogate my ex-girlfriend from high school. I'm the county sheriff, Adele, but I can't do my job, I can't keep you safe, if you don't give me information in a timely manner. I want to see you be a good reporter, not a *dead* one."

Adele spit out her words between clenched teeth.

"Roland wouldn't hurt me."

Lucas held out his hands with his palms facing upward in front of him.

"How can you say that, Adele? You don't even know him! And what about this Sergei? What kind of business is Roland doing with a Russian who goes around threatening women?"

"I don't know yet, but I intend to find out."

Lucas gently placed a hand on Adele's shoulder.

"Hold on, you can't go running around here messing with someone like Sergei. Let me do my job. I'll locate him, bring him in, and go from there. And if there's a connection to something illegal going on with Roland, I'll find that out, too."

Adele brushed away the sheriff's hand.

"No, you let me do *my* job, Lucas. This is a news story, and I intend to get to the truth."

Lucas turned around and kicked the dirt with the toe of his tennis shoe.

"All due respect, Adele, but you're not working for the *New York Times*. It's just the *Island Gazette*. That job isn't worth risking your own safety."

Adele's nostrils flared as she glared back at Lucas.

"And you're a little do-nothing sheriff more afraid of *losing* his job than he is of actually *doing* it!"

The sheriff wagged a finger in front of Adele's face.

"You don't know what I'm doing regarding the investigation. I don't tell you everything because I can't."

Adele's response was a thin, hard smile.

"Right back at you, Lucas. That makes two of us."

"What's that supposed to mean? What aren't you telling me?"

Adele pushed past the sheriff on her way toward the road leading back to Roche Harbor. Lucas had to jog to keep up.

"Adele, if you know something, you need to tell me."

Adele ignored the sheriff's plea and continued on her way.

"Don't make me bring you in!"

It was a threat Adele did not intend to go unchallenged. She whirled around to face the sheriff, her voice echoing off the trees just as the first drops of rain began to fall from the sky.

"You worry about doing your job, Lucas, and I'll do the same, and we'll see who gets to the truth first, OK? I'm not concerned about pissing off the county council with bad news or keeping secret whatever happened between you and Ophelia or engaging in power games with Roland. A young woman was murdered. Her body was hacked up and thrown into the sea. I'm gonna find out who did it. You can either help me, or you can get out of my way."

Adele could feel Lucas's eyes on her as she resumed her departure. She refused to look back. The air was thick with the scent of the sea. Droplets of rain grew in size and frequency as thunder shook the hard-packed ground beneath Adele's feet, and the trees above swayed slowly to the silent music of the increasing wind. The summer storm had arrived.

17.

By the time Adele neared her boat slip, her clothes were soaked. The skies had opened up, dropping a deluge of rainfall over the San Juan Islands. Just as she was about to turn left on the dock and make her way to her sailboat, she saw a familiar figure walking several yards in front of her on his way toward the northern half of the marina, where most of the largest and most expensive boats were slipped.

"Roland?"

Roland, holding a black umbrella in his right hand and wearing a light-blue jacket and black slacks, turned around looking slightly confused, and then his eyes widened as he recognized who had spoken his name.

"Adele! I just left your sailboat. I was going to invite you to my yacht for a bit of brunch and storm watching. The waters are going to get pretty snotty over the next few hours, and they're even forecasting some lightning."

Roland realized how wet Adele was and moved quickly to provide her cover under his umbrella.

"What are you doing out in this mess?"

Adele didn't want to talk about Lucas Pine, especially not with Roland Soros.

"I guess I picked a bad morning for a walk, huh?"

Roland pointed toward the back half of the marina.

"So, what do you say? Want to watch the storm with me?"

Perhaps it was fatigue or some residual resentment from her recent argument with Lucas, but Adele agreed to go with Roland to his yacht despite her misgivings about doing so.

Roland placed his arm around her shoulders to help keep her warm during the short walk to his yacht, while simultaneously trying to keep the worsening wind from ripping the umbrella out of his hands.

Adele could feel the dock rocking beneath her feet as waves began to splash over the sides, leaving small puddles along the marina's primary walkway. Roland's eyes gleamed with excitement.

"Wow, this might be the best storm we get this summer! My grandmother would bring me down here when I was a kid. We both loved to watch the waters churning, the whitecaps, the wind howling, and the lightning! That was *always* the best part. Like God was throwing a little temper tantrum just for us."

The Burger motor yacht's seventy-five-foot-long shimmering frame loomed just ahead of Adele and Roland. A stepped aluminum gangway attached to its side provided access from the dock to the vessel.

"There she is, the *Branch Office*. My grandfather named her. I suppose it was his attempt at a bit of banker's humor. Here, let me help you inside."

Roland took Adele by the hand and carefully guided her up the gangplank steps until she was safely aboard. She marveled at the mass of polished brass fixtures, stained mahogany decks, and the flawless white paint covering the ship's hull and superstructure.

"It must cost a small fortune to keep something like this looking so perfect. Everything shines like it's brand new."

"Yeah, it's not cheap, and I've thought of putting her up for sale many times but haven't quite been able to follow through. Not yet, anyways."

The ship's side walkway was fully covered and led to a heavily framed sliding door near the vessel's helm. With a grunt, Roland pulled the door open and then motioned for Adele to step inside.

As impressive as the yacht's exterior was, the interior was even more so. It was an immaculate display of gleaming wood floors, intricately designed throw rugs, and custom-made old-world-styled furnishings that would have looked at home within the finest luxury hotel.

"Geez, Roland, this is incredible."

Roland didn't respond, seeming slightly embarrassed by the trappings of his family's considerable financial success—success he had inherited.

Adele's eyes fell upon the many framed photographs that hung from the walls of the main sitting area that dominated the middle of the ship's upper-level living space. Most were black and white and dated back to the 1960s and '70s. Adele's mouth dropped open as she realized she recognized one of the most famous faces in modern American history within a photograph that had been placed prominently in the middle of all the others.

"Is that John F. Kennedy reading a book on the bow of this boat?"

Adele leaned in closer so she could read the date, which indicated the photo had been taken in September of 1960. The book in the then soon-to-be president's hands was Harper Lee's *To Kill a Mockingbird*. Kennedy wore a thick, dark-wool turtleneck sweater and appeared to be squinting from the sun shining in his eyes.

"Who took that photo?"

"Now *that's* a story my grandmother would share with just about everyone who came aboard. It was Mrs. Kennedy who borrowed Grandma's camera and took the picture. Apparently, she joked that her husband Jack was only holding the book for show because he thought it would make him appear more intellectual to the voters."

Adele looked from Roland to the picture of JFK and then back to Roland, who in turn chuckled at Adele's ongoing disbelief of what she was seeing.

"It was after a political fundraiser. Grandfather was friends with Senator Scoop Jackson, who lived about two hours south of here in Everett. It was the senator who set it up, probably as a way of thanking my grandfather for his campaign donations. Mr. Kennedy and his wife flew up to Roche Harbor by seaplane, did a little meet and greet with my grandparents and Senator Jackson, had something to eat, and then flew off. My grandfather had assured everyone he would deliver the island vote to Kennedy. I guess he made good on the promise."

Adele looked toward the bow of the boat.

"Is it OK if . . ."

Roland already knew she wanted to see the very location on the yacht depicted in the photo.

"Sure, c'mon. Oh, it's the same chair by the way."

Adele was once again frozen in disbelief.

"The same chair in the photo is still out there? The one Kennedy sat in?"

Roland's nod was accompanied by a twinkly-eyed smile.

"Yeah, the exact same one."

Adele was brought to the piece of furniture in question, a varnished lounge chair that sat underneath a large patio umbrella that managed to keep most of the rain off it, even as the wind blowing across the bow gusted with enough force Adele was pushed back a step. Adele, wide-eyed, pointed at the chair.

"May I?"

Roland chuckled.

"Yeah, of course, have at it."

Adele walked to the middle of the yacht's long bow and sat down on the chair. She remained there for several seconds with her eyes closed as the wind buffeted her hair across her face. With a deep breath, Adele stood up and gave Roland a shake of her head.

"Well, I didn't see this one coming. I just got to sit in a JFK chair! Roland Soros, you are one interesting man."

A crackling streak of lightning detonated somewhere to the north and was quickly followed by an angry retort of thunder.

"We better get inside, Adele. This storm show is about to get good!"

Roland turned up the ship's interior heat and handed Adele a blanket.

"Have a seat on the couch and a look out those windows. We can watch the big waves in the channel from here. I'll fix us up something to eat. You mind if I turn on some music?"

Adele gave a quick nod as she wrapped the blanket around her.

"Sure."

Roland used a remote he took off the granite kitchen counter to turn on the yacht's state-of-the-art sound system, and soon Adele was surrounded by the music of The Pogues as they sang, appropriately enough, of a rainy night in Soho, when the wind was whistling all its charms. Roland's own voice mixed with that of Irish singer Shane MacGowan.

Adele was surprised by how well Roland was able to carry a tune as he set about preparing a tray of cheese and crackers and mixing up a carafe of vodka and orange juice. Lastly, he grabbed two glass tumblers, which he had been chilling in the fridge.

"OK, we can have a bit of food and some screwdrivers and watch the storm."

Roland set the tray and carafe on the intricately hand-carved coffee table and then dropped down onto the dark leather couch directly next to Adele. He filled each of their glasses and then lifted his own glass in front of him.

"I propose a toast to new relationships and better days ahead."

Adele lightly tapped her drink against Roland's.

"I'll drink to that."

Over the course of the next thirty minutes, all of the food and much of the alcohol was consumed as the wind and rain buffeted the yacht's exterior. Roland engaged in superficial small talk as Adele listened politely, smiling and nodding her head when she thought it appropriate.

And then, as Roland likely knew she would, Adele took the conversation beyond mere niceties.

"I was told you were planning on building a casino out at Cattle Point. Is that true?"

Roland refilled the tumblers with the last of the orange juice and vodka and stood up.

"If we're going to have *that* kind of conversation, might I suggest another round of drinks?"

Adele was already well on her way to a rather nice, gentle alcohol-induced buzz, and felt only slightly guilty over it being still relatively early in the day.

"Sure, but don't think getting me drunk is going to detour me from getting answers, Mr. Soros."

Roland laughed.

"Oh, it's back to Mr. Soros again! I see the intrepid reporter will not be distracted from her duties."

Roland returned with the replenished carafe and set it on the coffee table. He sat down, lifted his glass to his mouth, and emptied half its contents before looking at Adele.

"I propose something a little different. I'll talk with you about my business, but it's off the record, and I want to have a little fun with it. What do you say?"

Adele knew Roland was most likely attempting to maintain control of their discussion. She sensed control was among the things he prized most above all else.

She looked at him across the brim of her glass and nodded. It was evident he liked her, and she intended to use that attraction to her advantage.

"What do you have in mind, Roland?"

Roland grinned.

"Oh, nothing complicated. I thought we might play some truth or dare."

Adele laughed.

"Really? You don't think we're a little old for that?"

Roland shook his head.

"One is never too old for the truth or a bit of daring."

Adele's face issued an exaggerated wince as her eyes shut tight.

"Is that a statement from Roland's rules for better living?"

Roland's smile was a relaxed gesture. He clearly didn't mind being teased by Adele.

"Something like that. Anyways, are you game?"

Adele emptied her tumbler and then held it up in front of her to be refilled.

"Sure, you go first. But you have to choose truth. Answer my question about you wanting to build a casino on the island."

Roland appeared satisfied with Adele's request.

"All right, I'll answer that as long as you promise this is all off the record."

Adele waved a dismissive hand in the air.

"Yeah-yeah, off the record, I promise."

Roland set his glass down and leaned back with his arms folded across his chest.

"The answer is yes. I *am* looking into building a comprehensive entertainment complex on the island that would include a casino, a world-class hotel, and a performing arts center."

Adele was about to ask a second question but was cut off as Roland wagged a finger in front of her face.

"No-no, it's *your* turn now. Truth or dare?"

After a few seconds' pause, Adele made her choice.

"Truth."

Roland refilled both their glasses and then continued with the game.

"Do you think I'm a good man?"

Adele's eyes widened as her mouth fell open.

"Uh, that's a difficult question to answer."

Roland shook his head.

"No, it's not. You agreed to play, so answer the question."

Adele took another drink as a way of giving herself a bit more time to come up with an appropriate response.

"I think you *could* be a good man, but I just don't know you well enough yet to be sure."

Both Adele and Roland flinched after an especially boisterous blast of thunder shook the walls of the yacht. A momentary frown from Roland revealed itself but was almost immediately replaced by another quick smile.

"Fair enough. I guess that just means we'll have to keep working on getting to know each other better."

Adele leaned forward, bringing her face closer to Roland's.

"Truth or dare?"

Roland stared into Adele's eyes.

"Dare."

Adele leaned back. She had already guessed Roland would choose that option next.

"I *dare* you to tell me the truth about what your relationship is with Sergei and why he threatened you. He said something about you having three more days. Three more days for what?"

Roland's face tightened.

"That's not how the game works, Adele."

Adele set her glass down.

"I disagree. I'm still daring you."

Roland's eyes drifted to the storm outside. The wind had started to diminish. When he looked back at Adele, it took more effort for him to smile, as if it almost hurt him to do so.

"I'll make an exception just this once. After I answer, you have to stick with one or the other. It's either truth or dare, understood?"

Adele nodded.

Roland sighed.

"My relationship with Sergei is nothing more than a simple matter of business. He is providing me access to some potential investment capital—seed money. That night in the parking lot after dinner, he was unhappy about a payment I've been disputing through him that he says is owed to some of his own business partners in Vancouver. These people like to keep their investment activity private. Sergei doesn't like the fact you're a reporter and has been agitated over my spending time with you. I assume he thinks I might say something that could compromise his ability to keep doing business with his Vancouver associates."

Adele made certain to focus on every word Roland spoke regarding Sergei, and then she worked just as hard to keep Roland talking, knowing one of the best ways to do that was to require that he defend a direct accusation made against him.

"Why are you working with organized crime, Roland? Why would you risk doing such a thing?"

Roland's eyes flashed a warning.

"You're pretty good at having our conversations end with me being angry at you, Adele, but I'm not going to let you do that this time. I know it's your nature to get to the truth, so I won't hold it against you. But the thing is I just told you the truth. Can't we just leave it at that and move on to another topic?"

"You told me *some* of the truth, Roland. I want to hear the rest."

"How about I tell you what *I* want, Adele? Or is this thing, whatever it is, just a one-way street, where you decide on the direction?"

Adele grabbed her drink and finished it off.

"Go ahead, Roland. What do you want?"

Roland emptied his glass as well.

"I want to finish the game, Adele. Truth or dare?"

Adele's eyes had grown heavy. The alcohol was taking hold.

"Dare."

Roland shifted on the couch so that he could place both his hands on Adele's shoulders.

"I dare you to kiss me."

Adele was surprised to hear the voice inside her head so forcibly cry out, *yes*. She wanted to kiss Roland—badly—though she wasn't entirely sure why. He was handsome, wealthy, and certainly mysterious, though doubts as to his true character remained.

He posed the question to me before, didn't he? Is Roland Soros a good man?

And then there was the matter of Lucas Pine, the equally attractive island golden boy turned county sheriff. Was he any better than Roland or, in fact, could he be something worse?

"Adele, I'm waiting. Do you accept the dare?"

Roland stared at Adele, the anticipation of the moment causing him to lightly run his tongue across his lips, an act that only intensified Adele's desire to feel his mouth and that tongue on her own. She leaned forward.

Roland responded in kind.

A blaring phone shattered the moment. Adele and Roland both recoiled, leaving an empty space between them thick with their shared, unfulfilled yearning. Though that same yearning was left unanswered, Adele's phone was not.

"Hello?"

It was Lucas.

"I just wanted to let you know we got Sergei. Border Patrol picked him up just before he crossed into Canadian waters on his boat. He's sitting in our holding cell now. We also confiscated a firearm he had with him. I'll be interrogating him first thing in the morning and will try to match his weapon with the bullet hole that was left in your vehicle. Would you be able to stop by the station tomorrow?"

Adele, still somewhat stunned and disappointed by the timing of the interruption, took a few seconds to focus her thoughts before she could respond.

"Uh, yeah, I can leave my car with you and then walk over to the newspaper office."

"Great, see you tomorrow."

Silence filled the uncomfortable void between reporter and sheriff.

"Is everything OK, Adele? You sound tired."

"Yeah, I'm fine. Guess that walk this morning wore me out a bit. I'll see you tomorrow."

The call was ended.

Roland's eyes bore into Adele.

"I take it that was our local sheriff picking the perfect time to interrupt us?"

Adele rubbed her eyes, trying to push back the drink-infused mental cobwebs cluttering her mind.

"Yes, that was Lucas."

Roland lightly scratched the stubble on his cheek.

"I just love it when you call him by his first name."

Almost as soon as he said it, Roland was again forcing himself to smile.

"Sorry, I'm not being fair to you. I'm just being jealous, and that's probably not something you want to deal with right now."

"Roland, you should know the sheriff just took Sergei into custody."

Roland sat completely still. The only thing that moved was a single blink of his eyes.

"He just told you that?"

"Yes. They found him with a weapon. They're going to try and match it to the bullet hole in my car."

"Adele, I told you he didn't shoot at you that night. I was there. You really think I would lie to you about that? Or that I would let him do such a thing?"

Adele's brow furrowed and her mouth tightened.

"I don't know exactly what happened that night, Roland. I'm just telling you what the sheriff told me because I thought you should know."

Roland stood up and moved toward the door before turning around and looking back at Adele.

"If you want, you can stay here until it stops raining. Make yourself at home."

"Where are you going?"

Roland's hands lifted from his sides.

"To get Sergei out of jail. Lucas Pine has no idea the shit storm he'll unleash if he keeps him in there."

Roland closed the door behind him, leaving Adele to sit alone in the yacht wondering what kind of trouble Roland intended for Lucas should he decide to keep Sergei in custody.

Outside, blue skies were slowly returning, an event marked by the unusually cheerful squall of a seagull flying overhead. More music filtered through the yacht, a haunting refrain by Jason Isbell that was the perfect accompaniment to the storm-after-the-storm moment Adele felt she was in.

She lay back on the couch, closed her eyes, and momentarily surrendered herself to both melody and chorus.

A heart on the run.
Keeps a hand on the gun.
You can't trust anyone . . .

18.

Adele awoke from a particularly deep slumber inside her sailboat to the sound of her cell phone demanding to be answered. She vaguely remembered walking back from Roland's yacht and lying down for what she intended to be just a brief nap.

That was nearly four hours ago.

"Hello?"

Avery's voice cut across the dull, static-cloud headache that dominated the space between Adele's ears.

"We just got a break on that dead body story, and it's *big*, Adele. We need you to come to the office ASAP."

Adele was about to end the call when she heard Avery start to say something more. She quickly brought the phone back to her ear.

"Oh, and Adele, if at all possible, avoid Sheriff Pine."

"What? Why?"

Avery lowered his voice to a near whisper.

"You'll see. Just get here as soon as you can."

It took Adele fewer than thirty minutes to take a quick shower, put on a fresh change of clothes, and make herself a cup of late-afternoon dark coffee. By the time she reached her car in the Roche Harbor parking lot, her hangover had lessened to little more than an easily manageable annoyance.

The drive to Friday Harbor was marked by sunny skies and much warmer temperatures than earlier in the day. When she reached the *Island Gazette* office, it was nearly five o'clock. Adele was surprised to find the front door locked. She gave it a light rap and then waited. Seconds later, the door was cracked open by just a few inches. Avery peered out from between the gap, confirmed it was Adele, and then opened the door farther.

"Hurry, come on in."

Once Adele was inside, he shut the door and locked it.

"Avery, what's this all about?"

Avery headed toward the back of the office without saying anything. Instead, he merely motioned with his hand for Adele to follow.

Once in the back room, Adele found Jose standing next to a young dark-skinned woman, who was sitting in a chair. Her eyes were wide as she clenched and unclenched hands that rested on top of her blue-jeaned thighs. Her shoulder-length dark hair was tied back from her smooth face, highlighting a pair of prominent cheekbones, full lips, and a long, delicate neck. Bess moved out from behind the old printing press and gave Adele a quick hug. She appeared almost as nervous as the young woman.

"Thank you for getting here so quickly, Adele."

Bess smiled at the woman sitting next to Jose.

"Paula, this is our friend and reporter Adele Plank. You can trust her, OK? Adele, this is Paula Mendoza. She works just down the road from us at the Crow's Nest."

Though she had not been there, Adele knew the Crow's Nest to be one of the more popular restaurant and lounges in Friday Harbor, particularly among the locals. It sat perched over the water some three hundred yards northeast of the ferry terminal, where it remained a waterfront fixture as it had for nearly forty years.

Jose spoke in Spanish to Paula, who listened intently. She looked up at Adele and gave a single nod of her head.

Bess placed a hand on Paula's shoulder.

"She's afraid to go to the police because of what she saw and also because she's not a legal citizen. Jose, have her repeat to Adele what she told us earlier."

Jose gave Paula a warm smile before communicating to her in Spanish. Paula looked at Adele again before her gaze returned to Jose. She began to speak, slowly at first, and then her words came more quickly, punctuated by her eyes further widening from time to time.

Jose then interpreted in English what was being said.

"She worked at the restaurant with a Russian girl named Nadia Orlov. Nadia started there about six months ago. She moved down from Vancouver and had just turned nineteen. They quickly became friends. Nadia spoke a little Spanish and taught Paula some Russian, and after a few weeks of hanging out at work, they decided to share an apartment in town together. Two weeks ago, Nadia disappeared. She didn't leave a note, phone message, or a text. Nothing—she just vanished."

Paula wiped near-frantic tears from her eyes before continuing.

"When she read the story about the body that was found near Ripple Island, she knew it was Nadia. She also thinks she knows who killed her. She saw him with her the last time she saw Nadia alive."

Adele looked up and found both Bess and Avery staring back at her. Jose cleared his throat as Paula said more.

"Nadia was in the lounge. She had finished her hostess shift a couple of hours earlier and was drinking heavily. The owners didn't know she was underage. Her ID was a fake and said she was twenty-two. Paula was doing dishes in the kitchen. It had been a busy night, so she was working late. It was past midnight when she walked into the lounge and saw Nadia speaking with a tall, good-looking man. He was clearly trying to get her to leave with him and seemed angry at her. Paula went back to the kitchen to finish the last of the dishes as fast as she could, but by the time she returned to the lounge both Nadia and the man were gone."

Jose paused, squeezed Paula's hand, and then continued.

"She read the last issue of the paper and saw a picture of the same man who was talking to Nadia that night. He wasn't in uniform the time she saw him with Nadia, but Paula is positive it was him. It was the sheriff."

Adele was quick to push back against the conspiracy that had so evidently formed inside the newspaper office against Lucas Pine.

"Hold on. How do we even know the body found near Ripple Island has anything to do with this Nadia? What if she just took off? Maybe she went back to Vancouver?"

Jose translated Adele's questions to Paula, who immediately shook her head. She responded in short, angry bursts.

"No, Paula says that's not what happened. She says Nadia won't answer her phone. That Nadia *always* answered her phone or a text and hasn't contacted her since that night. She never came home from work. Paula thinks Nadia left with the sheriff, and then she disappeared."

Adele forced her mind to clear itself of unnecessary clutter. She needed to focus entirely on the possibility that Lucas might very well have something to do with the missing woman.

As much as I don't want to believe it, I have to go where the evidence points.

"Jose, can you ask Paula if some of Nadia's things are still in her apartment—like a hairbrush?"

Jose did as Adele asked. Paula indicated to him Nadia's belongings still remained in the apartment.

"OK, good. I need you to return there with her, put the brush into a plastic bag, and bring it here. And, Jose, make sure you wear gloves. Don't get your prints on the brush or the bag, understand?"

Jose nodded and then left with Paula, leaving Adele to face the accusatory looks of both Avery and Bess Jenkins. Bess was first to speak.

"I know you consider Lucas Pine your friend, Adele, and frankly we find it hard to believe ourselves, but if he *did* have something to do with that girl's disappearance, we need to find out."

Avery chimed in as well.

"That's right. The story will lead where it leads, and it's our job to take it to its truthful conclusion, even if it means going after one of our own. This is, after all, something that involves a young woman's murder."

Adele sighed.

"I know. Don't worry. I'll go where the truth leads me, although I'm not going to assign guilt just yet. Paula's evidence is circumstantial at best."

"It might not be enough to convict anyone in a court of law, but it's more than enough for a news story. The public has a right to know."

Adele turned toward Avery. She wasn't about to give up any of her control over the developing story.

"Give me just a few days, Avery. We're not going to print until next week. I need a little time to confirm what Paula shared and give Lucas the opportunity to respond."

Avery's mouth fell downward into a deep, troubled frown.

"You mean give the sheriff the chance to defend himself, to change your mind, and try and bury the story?"

Though she remained respectful of the longtime newspaper owner, Adele held firm in her belief the story was not yet ready to be shared with the public.

"If we go after Sheriff Pine with something half-baked and are proven in the end to have been wrong, the damage to the newspaper's reputation will be far greater than the short-term bump the initial story would provide. We do this my way, Avery, or I won't be involved at all. As you just said, the accusation is one of murder. The stakes couldn't be higher or our responsibility any greater."

Avery opened his mouth to object but was cut off by his wife.

"Adele is right. We need to be very careful how we proceed with this. If we get this wrong, it could destroy the paper. Everything you worked for, it could all be gone. Give her the few days to follow up on this new information."

Avery looked at Bess and then at Adele. He finally gave in to their demand for more time with an exaggerated shrug of his shoulders. He then held up three fingers.

"I'll give you your three days, Adele, but after that, I'm running the story, with or without your input."

Adele nodded.

"I understand, Avery, and thank you."

Jose returned with a brown-handled hairbrush inside a plastic ziplock bag. His right hand was still enclosed in a latex glove, per Adele's instructions. He dropped the bagged brush onto the table where Avery's computer sat and then explained that Paula intended to leave for the mainland on the next ferry out of Friday Harbor. She would remain with family until she felt it safe to return.

Jose took out his phone and pulled up a selfie that showed Paula posing with a beautiful brown-haired young woman in front of the Roche Harbor Hotel. Adele was struck by the brilliant blue of the woman's eyes.

"That's Nadia. Paula wanted you to see her as a living human being, not merely as some random person who has gone missing. I've already e-mailed the picture to all of you."

Adele took Jose's phone into her hands and stared into Nadia Orlov's azure orbs that were so similar to the deep dark waters into which her friend Paula feared her body had been dumped.

"You can tell Paula I'll do everything I can to find out what happened to Nadia, Jose."

Jose took his phone back as he nodded to Adele, then he turned and left the office.

Bess pointed to the hairbrush.

"So, what do you intend to do with *that*?"

Adele stared down at the brush, knowing her answer was likely to stun and confuse the old couple.

"I'm going to hand it over to Lucas Pine."

19.

The following morning:

"Sheriff, it's not a match. I'm almost positive that hole was left by a .45 caliber. As you already know, the weapon you confiscated off the fella you're holding inside, fires 9-millimeter rounds."

Lucas rubbed the side of his head. Sergei's lawyer was due to arrive at any moment, and now the sheriff had nothing to keep the Russian locked up and away from Adele.

"Are you absolutely positive, Gunther?"

Texas-born Deputy Gunther Fox was a thirty-six-year military veteran who had until a few years ago spent four years volunteering as a reserve officer for the Seattle Police Department to supplement his military pension. After moving with his wife to the San Juan Islands to retire, he was contacted personally by Sheriff Pine and asked to join the revamped San Juan County Sheriff's Office. Gunther detested life without work so was quick to accept.

He was a short, powerfully built, gray-mustached man of sixty-four years who had quickly garnered a no-nonsense reputation regarding how he carried out his island law enforcement duties. Lucas had assigned Gunther to the Lopez Island substation, an almost perpetually low-key affair that had his days most often occupied with making certain the island's multitude of bicyclists were given the proper right-of-way by those driving around the island in their cars. Lopez was where Gunther had his home with his wife of thirty-three years, Melinda, who he had first met when they were both serving in the marines.

"I've investigated thousands of rounds over a whole lot of years, Sheriff. I'm about as sure as I can be without having the actual round or casing to do further ballistics on. I think you already figured that yourself but was hoping I'd give you different news."

The sheriff gave a frustrated nod.

"Yeah, you got that right. How about you, Chancee? Have an opinion?"

Twenty-five-year-old Deputy Chancee Smith was the third member of the three-person department that comprised the entirety of the San Juan County Sheriff's Office. She had a two-year degree in criminal justice and just recently completed the Basic Law Enforcement Academy on the other side of Washington State in Spokane. She had been one of six applicants Lucas had interviewed for the position at the Orcas Island substation. He gave her the job not because he knew she was the most qualified law enforcement officer who applied, but rather because she was willing to admit she still had a lot to learn. Chancee made it clear she simply wanted to be the best law enforcement officer possible. She was slight of stature but big of heart and totally dedicated to helping others, and that was enough to convince Lucas to give her the chance to prove she would be a good fit within the department.

"I'll have to defer to Deputy Fox, Sheriff. If he says it was a .45 caliber that left the hole, that's good enough for me. I'd just note that you don't see .45 rounds used nearly as much these days. Makes me wonder if it was an older weapon that was fired at Ms. Plank's vehicle."

Lucas turned to Adele, who had been silently watching the discussion from a few paces away.

"I'm sorry, Adele, I can't keep him in custody any longer. At least we'll have made his fancy lawyer fly out here from Bellingham for nothing. By the time he arrives, Sergei will be long gone already."

"I understand, Sheriff. You have to do what's right—and legal."

The sheriff nodded his head at Chancee.

"Deputy, please release Mr. Kozlov, and bring him out here."

Gunther Fox folded his arms across his broad chest and muttered a few choice curse words under his breath.

"This Sergei might not have been the one to shoot at Ms. Plank's car, but he stinks like a criminal, no matter what his record says. It also means that if Sergei didn't take that shot, someone else sure as hell did, and that someone is still out there."

The front door to the sheriff's department was flung open. Sergei walked out with his shoulders set back and his chin held high. He scoffed at the scowling faces of Sheriff Pine and Deputy Fox.

"Next time I file harassment charges, you stupid hick cops. I told you I have nothing to do with shooting at anyone."

Sergei's eyes settled on Adele.

"As for *you*, I said I see you again, and I will. Count on it."

Lucas's hand shot out like a striking cobra and grabbed the front of Sergei's dark-gray sweatshirt.

"Hey! Was that a threat? If it was, I'll throw your ass right back in there!"

Sergei's eyes flared. The fire within them quickly diminished to a low simmer as he pushed the sheriff's hand away from him.

"It isn't crime to *see* someone, Sheriff. She's pretty girl. I might want to pay that kind of pretty a visit, is all."

The sheriff pulled back his clenched right fist, fully prepared to send it crashing into Sergei's smirking face. Gunther pushed himself between the two men, trying to prevent a potentially disastrous altercation that would likely cause the sheriff considerable legal trouble.

"How about you take your Vancouver candy ass on out of here, Mr. Kozlov. You caught a break—this time. Don't push it. Oh, and we *will* be recommending charges be filed against you with the prosecutor for carrying an unlicensed firearm, which we'll also be keeping, by the way."

Sergei straightened his sweatshirt and chuckled while wagging a finger at Lucas.

"You'll have an election coming up soon enough, Sheriff. Don't be surprised if certain people around here decide it best you no longer wear that shiny little badge of yours."

The sheriff growled his words between tightly clenched teeth. Adele sensed how badly Lucas wanted to tear the Russian's limbs apart.

"Guess it's too bad for you that you can't vote."

Sergei's smile took on shark-like proportions, his thick accent complimenting the predatory hue of his face.

"Hmmm, I wouldn't count on *that*, Sheriff. Where there's will, there's *always* way. You take care now."

Adele watched as Sergei drove off in the same black pickup truck she had seen him in days earlier. He pulled onto the road slowly and honked his horn while waving at the sheriff and the others, an act that was followed by Chancee waving back at the Russian with her own middle finger salute.

"If I ever have to shoot someone on the job, I don't think I'd mind too much if it was him."

Lucas shook the hands of his deputies and thanked them for making the trip to Friday Harbor. Both Chancee and Gunther indicated they would be returning to their respective Orcas and Lopez island substations within the hour. Before leaving, Gunther pointed at Lucas.

"You make sure to try and avoid that Sergei, Sheriff. A man like him *wants* trouble. It's what motivates them. He might have been all smiles and waves on the outside, but having to sit in that cell overnight . . . he's plenty pissed off about it. He'd like nothing more than to see your career go down in flames."

A moment later found the sheriff and Adele standing alone on the sidewalk in front of the sheriff's office. White, puffy clouds moved slowly overhead, and in the distance Adele heard the sound of someone mowing their lawn.

"You said you had something to show me?"

Adele nodded.

"Yeah, you're going to want to see this inside your office."

Lucas gave Adele a quizzical look, wondering what it was she wanted him to see.

"Sure, right this way."

Adele followed the sheriff into his office. He closed the door, asked that Adele take a seat, and then sat down as well behind his desk.

"So, what's this about?"

Adele removed the plastic bag holding the hairbrush from the inside of her jacket. She placed it on the desk and pushed it toward the sheriff.

"You'll want to compare the DNA from the hair on that brush with the bones you found inside the crab pot near Ripple Island."

The sheriff's brows lifted over widened eyes. Those same eyes moved back and forth between the brush and Adele.

"You think it'll be a match?"

Adele folded her hands underneath her chin while resting her elbows on the edge of the desk.

"It might."

"And how would you know that? Who does the brush belong to?"

Adele made certain to keep her face as unreadable as possible, while at the same time focusing intensely on Lucas's own reaction.

"It belongs to a young woman. Her roommate thinks she has gone missing. Actually, she thinks she's dead."

"You mean she thinks the woman who owned that brush is the same one whose remains were pulled from the water?"

Adele nodded.

"Yes."

Lucas leaned back in his chair and took the next several seconds to stare silently back at Adele. When next he spoke, Adele sensed something different in his voice. It wasn't fear or confusion, but rather a subtle hint of concern over his inability to see where Adele might be leading him. Whether that concern was for her or for himself she couldn't yet tell.

"I'll need to interview this roommate."

"No, Lucas, what you need to do is get the hair on that brush DNA tested as soon as possible."

The sheriff clasped his hands together atop his desk and leaned forward.

"Are we on the same side here, Adele, or are you fighting me for some reason?"

Adele didn't allow herself to wither under the intensity of the young sheriff's gaze.

"I'm on the side of truth, Lucas, and when I find it, I hope to find you there as well."

Lucas smiled. His eyes did not.

"You don't dictate the terms of *my* investigation, Ms. Plank."

"And you don't dictate the terms of *my* reporting, Sheriff Pine."

"I could arrest you for obstruction."

"You wouldn't."

This time the sheriff's eyes revealed a hint of humor in them.

"I could, but I won't—not *yet*. I'll fly to Seattle this afternoon with that brush, have it tested first thing tomorrow morning, and compare the results to those of the remains. If there *is* a match, you and I will be having ourselves a very serious and honest discussion about what you'll need to do next."

Adele straightened in her chair and issued the sheriff a faint smile.

"If there's a match, you're right. We *will* be having ourselves a discussion. How serious and honest will be entirely up to you."

The sheriff's penetrating glare continued to seek the answers to the mystery of the hairbrush that Adele seemed so certain was connected to the Ripple Island investigation. She remained as unreadable as a world-class poker player.

But even the greatest card player will sometimes overplay their hand.

Lucas abruptly stood up, and with a single stride stood next to the door and partially opened it. Adele got up from her chair and reached out to open the door farther so that she could step out into the adjacent hallway but found the sheriff holding onto the door and preventing her from doing so.

"I don't suppose you'll at least tell me if the roommate is still in town?"

Though she knew Paula was likely already gone from the island, Adele thought it best to keep that information to herself.

"No, I won't."

With one hand Lucas continued to stop the door from moving, while rubbing the back of his neck with the other.

"Open the door, Sheriff."

Lucas shook his head and grinned.

"I'm wondering if I *should* arrest you, just to teach you a lesson. Might do you some good."

"Sheriff, Mark Twain once said a person should never pick a fight with someone who buys ink by the barrel. Around here, that someone is me and the *Island Gazette*."

"That sounds like something Roland Soros would say."

Adele's eyes rolled skyward.

"For crying out loud, Lucas, this isn't about a competition with Roland, where you seem to think I'm some prize to be shuffled between the two of you. Maybe we should get him down here, have him stand right next to you, and then you can both drop your pants and let me decide from there who the *real* winner is!"

The sheriff cocked one brow, surprised by Adele's sudden outburst. He stepped back from the door and allowed her to open it fully on her way into the hallway. She was nearly to the exit when Lucas's voice called out her name, causing her to turn around.

The sheriff used his shoulder to lean against the wall as his eyes appraised Adele with a hawkish gleam.

"I just wanted you to know, that contest you proposed between me and Roland . . . I'm pretty sure I'd measure up just fine."

Adele folded her arms across her chest and gave the sheriff a look of withering disdain that was only partly exaggerated.

"I wouldn't be so confident about that. In fact, I think you might be selling Roland short."

Adele watched with more than a little satisfaction as Lucas's mouth fell open. Having delivered a decisive blow to the sheriff's ego, she quickly exited the building.

Once outside, the momentary humor fell away and was replaced by Adele's concern that Lucas Pine might possibly be implicated in the death of Nadia Orlov. She still refused to believe it likely, trusting the instincts that informed her Lucas was, in fact, a good man. Adele then recalled another troubling piece to the morning's revelations, as told by Deputy Gunther Fox.

If Sergei didn't take that shot, someone else sure as hell did, and that someone is still out there.

Adele looked out at the bustling human throng that was Friday Harbor and wondered if that same someone was watching her at that very moment, waiting and plotting for the right time to take another shot.

20.

It was just past two o'clock in the afternoon when Adele answered a phone call from Roland Soros. Lucas Pine had already flown out of Friday Harbor ten minutes earlier on his way to Seattle to have the DNA test done on Nadia Orlov's hairbrush.

"I have something I think you'll want to see."

Adele pulled her car over to the side of the road next to an open field of tall grass, some three miles south of Roche Harbor.

"What is it?"

Roland answered in a whisper, not wanting to be overheard. Adele could hear people talking in the background.

"It involves someone named Nadia Orlov. She's employed by a business that leases space from a building I own."

"The Crow's Nest."

Roland didn't sound surprised Adele already knew the name of the restaurant.

"That's right. I take it you already spoke with another employee there named Paula Mendoza?"

Adele attempted to take control of the conversation by asking Roland a question instead of merely answering his.

"How do you know Paula Mendoza?"

"I was given the name by the owner of the Crow's Nest. She had come in asking to see surveillance footage. I have cameras set up throughout the building. The owner contacted me to let me know about the request. That's when he also told me that this Paula was worried Nadia was missing."

Adele's mind quickly connected the dots between what she had already been told by Paula Mendoza and Roland's sudden request to show her something.

"You have footage of Lucas with Nadia Orlov."

Roland's tone was devoid of any pleasure in his confirmation of that fact.

"Yes. As I said, I think you'll want to see this. I'm at the Crow's Nest now. The owner won't talk to you, so don't ask. He wants nothing to do with any of this. I own the building and the surveillance equipment, so, ultimately, the footage is mine. He has no choice but to let me show it to you. There's an entrance to the back office just past the green dumpsters. I'll leave the door unlocked."

Within twenty minutes, Adele was pulling open the door that had been left unlocked, just as Roland indicated it would be. He stood inside a dimly lit, low-ceilinged hall and motioned for Adele to follow him into an adjacent office.

Once they were both inside, Roland closed the door behind them and locked it. A stained oak desk was to their left, on which sat a computer monitor and keyboard. A single lamp on the right corner of the desk provided the only light to the windowless space. The aged green carpet was badly worn and frayed in several places.

As Roland sat down, the dark hues of his slacks and dress shirt made him appear to disappear into the inky vinyl that covered the office chair. Adele stood directly to his right as they both stared at the computer screen, which clearly showed Lucas Pine sitting at the Crow's Nest bar next to Nadia Orlov.

Nadia still wore her hostess uniform, a white dress shirt and black skirt, while Lucas was clothed in a red T-shirt and blue jeans. Adele was quick to note a half-full drink sat in front of Nadia, while Lucas didn't appear to be drinking.

Roland rewound the footage to the moment where Lucas first sat down next to the young Russian woman.

"Is there audio?"

Roland shook his head.

"No, just visual. I'll play the entire portion that shows them together. It's about two minutes."

Adele fixed her eyes upon the images playing out before her. She watched as Lucas first stood behind Nadia and said something that caused the hostess to look up at the sheriff. The Russian frowned. Lucas sat down to her left and pointed at the glass in Nadia's hand. Nadia shook her head. Lucas appeared to straighten on the bar stool, and then he folded his arms across his chest while saying something that caused Nadia to shrug and shake her head again.

Roland pointed at the screen.

"Watch this."

Lucas placed his hand around the back of Nadia's arm. She appeared to shout something as she pulled away. Lucas stood up and proceeded to again place his hand on Nadia's arm and looked ready to forcibly pull her off the bar stool, but instead he leaned down closer to her and said something that caused the young woman to start laughing. Nadia stood up smiling, and then both she and the sheriff left the bar together.

Roland stopped the digital video, took in a deep breath, and then unleashed a long sigh, while Adele pondered the possibilities of what the footage depicted.

"She was underage. He could have simply been citing her."

Roland's thin, pained smile indicated he had already considered that same scenario and found it unlikely.

"Maybe, but he wasn't in uniform, so he wasn't on duty. And what if the body that was found was, in fact, Nadia Orlov? If Lucas was the last one to be seen with her . . ."

Roland's words trailed off, the silence saying more than words could.

"Yes, it looks bad, but it doesn't prove anything. I don't believe Lucas had anything to do with Nadia Orlov's alleged disappearance. He's *not* a killer."

Roland again pointed at the computer screen.

"The fact it looks bad is all that might be needed to have the county council shut down the department. It's certainly enough to open an investigation against Lucas. Fewer and fewer people will want us to maintain local control of our police force. It'll all be handed over to the state."

"Which means you'll lose control, too, isn't that right, Roland? I can't help but think your concern for Lucas is secondary to your concern you might have state officials running around your backyard checking into everyone's business—including your own."

Roland was about to object but was cut off by Adele.

"Nadia is, or *was*, Russian by way of Vancouver, same as Sergei. Is it your intention I'm supposed to forget all about *that* particular coincidence in light of this video footage you just showed me?"

Roland's mouth tightened as he considered the extent of Adele's accusation.

"So, you want to ignore what you just saw and instead try and somehow implicate *me* in that young woman's disappearance?"

"No, Roland, what I'm saying is that there is a lot more to this story than that video footage shows. This is twice you've pointed me in Lucas's direction. I'm reminding you there's plenty I could use to just as easily point an investigation at you as well."

Roland made certain Adele didn't have the opportunity to interrupt him again. The volume of his voice was akin to a verbal hand that covered her mouth, telling her to shut up and listen.

"Dammit, Adele, I'm not trying to implicate Lucas! I'm trying to protect him! If state investigators do come here, they will find out he might have been the last person to see her alive, and Lucas will be in a world of hurt because of it. This could happen not in a matter of weeks but days if we aren't able to figure out what exactly happened to that young woman and who was responsible. Whatever rivalry Lucas and I might have regarding our feelings toward you has no bearing on my wanting to keep him on as sheriff."

"Because that's what's best for your business, right?"

Roland nodded.

"Yeah, and it's also what's best for the people who call these islands their home. There's something different, something unique about this place. I know you feel the same. Things are better here for a reason. It's the people molded to the geography and vice versa. If we hand it over to outsiders, it'll never be the same. We'll lose it, and in the process we'll lose ourselves."

"And yet you want to bring in thousands of outsiders each month by way of a Cattle Point casino complex."

Roland shrugged.

"That's right. Change is inevitable. The only question that remains is who will control it. I intend to make certain it's *me*, because I'm the one most capable of keeping the uniqueness of these islands intact. We'll invite the future here, entertain it, take its money, and then send it on its way."

Adele saw more clearly than ever the juxtaposition of love for the San Juan Islands and the yearning for future financial success that was the primary fuel that burned so strongly within Roland Soros. She wondered if he realized how perilously close he was to giving up his own self-control to that fire or if he would even care.

"I'd like a copy of that footage. E-mail it to me."

The corners of Roland's mouth curled upward as he realized Adele hadn't request the footage from him; she had demanded it.

"Of course, you'll have it within the hour."

Adele moved toward the door. She expected to hear Roland's voice stopping her with another question or comment, but he remained seated and silent. When she looked back, she was the one who spoke, not him.

"Within the hour?"

Roland gave Adele a thin smile and nod.

"Yes, within the hour."

The outside air was heavy with both the scent and feel of saltwater, signifying high humidity that almost immediately caused a layer of sweat to form across Adele's forehead.

Her eyes followed the sound of the fluttering black-and-green Crow's Nest flag that hung over the entrance to the restaurant. The sky was a vast, cloudless dome with no hint of the recent storm.

Adele's head snapped to the left. She was certain of being watched but found the sidewalk behind her empty. A familiar voice rang out from across the street.

"Dr. Pine, what are you doing out here all by yourself?"

Adele followed the voice and saw Ophelia Norris straddling the same ten-speed bicycle Adele had first seen just outside Ophelia's Cattle Point home. Ophelia stood on the sidewalk in front of a clearly bewildered Edmund Pine. Lucas's father wore a long navy blue bathrobe and matching slippers. Ophelia's blonde hair was tied in the back and partially hidden underneath a yellow bike helmet.

"Where is Lucas, Dr. Pine?"

The doctor backed away from Ophelia, his eyes darting wildly from side to side. His mouth opened and closed, wanting to form words his addled mind could not create. Adele jogged across the street until she stood next to the doctor.

"Dr. Pine, it's Adele. Remember me?"

Edmund initially glared at Adele, but within seconds his eyes softened as a grateful smile pushed outward from both sides of his mouth.

"Hello, young lady! You're Lucas's friend!"

The doctor's smile dissipated, replaced by a narrow-eyed scowl.

"I've been looking for Lucas. I walked and walked and walked, but I can't seem to find where he is. Can you help me find him?"

Ophelia's voice severed Adele's response before it could start.

"You're the newspaper lady, the one who came out to my place. You know Dr. Pine?"

Adele nodded.

"Yes, Lucas introduced us."

Ophelia's eyes raked over Adele as if she were suspicious of Adele's claim of actually knowing the doctor.

"You have your car and with you and able to get him home safely?"

"Sure, I'll drive him there now."

Ophelia's suspicion turned to gratitude. She gave the doctor a warm smile.

"Take care of yourself, Dr. Pine. Your friend here is going to make sure you get back home safe, OK?"

Ophelia gave Adele a curt nod and then took off down the road on her bike without looking back, her powerful legs soon propelling her to nearly twenty miles an hour.

"Have you seen my son? I think it's almost dinnertime. He's going to go without his supper."

Adele felt one of the doctor's hands gently tugging on the sleeve of her sweatshirt.

"Let me take you home, Dr. Pine. I'm sure Lucas will be back soon."

The doctor beamed like a happy child opening new presents on Christmas.

"Yes, he has always been such a good boy."

Adele hoped Lucas's father was right even as she quietly admitted to herself that she was no longer so certain.

21.

It was the sound of slow-moving footsteps that woke Adele from her place on the couch in the sitting room of the Pine residence. Edmund Pine had descended the stairs and was looking at her with a bemused smile on his deeply lined face. He was neatly dressed in a light-gray suit matched with a crisp white dress shirt and blood-red tie.

"Did you sleep there all night?"

Adele sat up and rolled her head from side to side, trying to work the kinks out of her neck.

"Yeah, guess I fell asleep."

The slight confusion in the doctor's eyes gave way to kind approval.

"I'll make us some fresh coffee."

When Adele had returned the doctor to his home the previous day, she found a panicked Maxine Foss waiting. The retired nurse who Lucas had earlier told Adele helped watch his father during the day, was a thickly built, middle-aged woman with especially expressive brown eyes housed behind a pair of thick-lensed glasses.

"Oh, my goodness, there you are Doctor!"

Maxine's face was stricken with both guilt and worry.

"Lucas called me saying he would be out of town. I was on the ferry coming back from Anacortes, and by the time I got here, the doctor was gone. I walked the neighborhood trying to find him and then waited here for him to come back. Thank you so much for returning him home."

Maxine then explained how she had an appointment that evening. Adele assured the former nurse she would be happy to stay and watch Edmund until he was safely in bed. Once the doctor had fallen asleep, Adele decided to get a quick nap herself—a nap that ultimately turned into a deep overnight slumber on the sitting room couch. Dr. Pine returned from the kitchen and announced the coffee was ready.

"You want to sit with me on the front porch while we drink it?"

Adele stood up and smiled.

"Sure."

Edmund Pine made the short walk back into the kitchen and then returned holding two porcelain cups, one of which he handed to Adele. She followed him outside and sat next to him on a porch swing he said was first put up shortly after Lucas was born.

"He loved to be held here, moving slowly back and forth. His mother must have logged a thousand hours with him on this swing."

The doctor went quiet as he stared out at the nearly empty street in front of his home. Adele could hear a myriad of bees buzzing about the many flowering plants that dotted the well-manicured property. Edmund's chin slowly dropped to his chest as he looked down into the black abyss that was his coffee cup.

"This is what Lucas calls a good morning for me, when I can think more clearly. What he doesn't understand is that with memory comes the pain of knowing what's gone. I'm losing my mind, and frankly I'd rather not be aware of it."

Edmund shifted in the swing's bench seat.

"Your name is Adele."

Adele nodded.

"That's right. You remember."

The doctor closed his eyes for a brief moment and then opened them.

"For now, yes. And yesterday, you were with, uh, Lucas's girlfriend. Her family lives over in . . . Cattle Point?"

"Yes, that was her on the bike."

Edmund's brow furrowed as he sat back in the porch swing.

"She was a patient of mine, you know. Lucas's mother had concerns about those two dating. It's a Jewish thing, the overprotective mother. And given Lucas was her only child, Katarina likely never thought anyone was good enough for her boy."

"You're talking about Ophelia Norris, right?"

The doctor took a sip of coffee and nodded.

"Yes, Ophelia. She was the cheerleader to Lucas's quarterback. But Katarina and Ophelia, that was more like oil and water. I should have seen the conflict between them coming, but by the time it arrived, it was too late. Could have caused quite a mess for poor Lucas right before he left for college. There's likely still a few around here who think they know the truth of what really happened. They don't, of course. It's all just rumor and gossip."

Adele lowered her cup, not certain Edmund Pine's recollections were accurate or muddled by his dementia. Edmund abruptly stood up and pointed toward the front door.

"Here, let me show you!"

The doctor led Adele back into the house and down a hallway to his study, where he then stood proudly smiling next to two framed doctorate degrees prominently displayed behind his desk. One was for medicine and the other psychiatry.

"It was a dual degree program from the University of California. I'm certified in both family medicine and psychiatry."

Adele leaned forward to look more closely at the psychiatry degree.

"Dr. Pine, were you Ophelia Norris's medical doctor or her psychiatrist?"

Edmund's eyes were thin slits as he cocked his head to the side.

"Who?"

"Ophelia Norris, the woman we saw on the bike yesterday. She dated Lucas in high school."

The doctor's eyes went blank for several seconds before suddenly widening.

"Oh, yes, of course! I was both. She was a beautiful young woman, but like so many would be in a similar circumstance, she had difficulty dealing with the separation that developed after Lucas accepted the scholarship to play football back East. He was leaving the islands. She was not. They argued about it a great deal during their senior year, and over time Katarina became more and more involved, understandably taking the side of her son, and in the end, Lucas, just as understandably, took the side of his mother."

"What happened between them, Dr. Pine? What was the thing that caused the rumors and gossip you mentioned?"

The doctor appeared ready to explain, but then issued a frowning shake of his head.

"No, that is privileged information between doctor and patient."

Edmund glanced at the open doorway in his study, seeming to think someone might be standing in the hallway.

"Plus, I promised Katarina I wouldn't mention it. She blames herself as much as anyone for what happened that terrible day. I wouldn't want to disappoint her by saying something now."

The doctor's eyes took on the same blank appearance as they had earlier. Edmund stood silent and motionless, staring at the wall directly behind Adele. He blinked several times, cleared his throat, and then smiled.

"Say, have you seen Katarina's roses? She takes such pride in her roses, as well she should. Would you like to see them?"

Adele was about to agree to walk back outside with Edmund when her eyes noted for the first time the revolver sitting on a brass mount atop a wood file cabinet behind the doctor's study door.

"Is that your gun?"

The doctor nodded as he took the weapon down from its place on the file cabinet and held it in his right hand.

"Yes, it's an old Colt 45 that's been in the family for three generations. It's the very weapon Lucas first learned to shoot with. I would take him to the old gravel pit in the middle of the island, and we'd use cans to target practice together. He couldn't have been more than, oh, eleven or twelve at the time. Like everything else involving hand-eye coordination, he was a natural and was soon a much better shot than I could ever hope to be."

"It's called a Colt 45 because it shoots .45-caliber bullets?"

Dr. Pine's mouth formed a fleeting frown.

"I suppose that's right, yes."

The doctor opened the top drawer of the file cabinet and looked inside, an act that caused his frown to become more pronounced.

"Hmmm, I always kept a box of bullets in here, but they appear to be missing."

Edmund closed the drawer and then lifted the gun toward Adele.

"Did you want to hold it?"

Adele shook her head.

"No, that's OK."

The doctor and Adele both looked up at the sound of the front door opening.

"Dad, you in here?"

It was Lucas, having returned from his trip to Seattle.

Edmund walked out into the hallway still holding the revolver.

"You're back from work already, son?"

The doctor appeared to be unaware Lucas hadn't come home the previous night.

The sheriff's alarmed reply echoed inside the house.

"Dad, what the hell are you doing with *that*?"

Adele stood behind the doctor and watched as he looked down at the gun in his hand.

"Oh, I was showing your friend, the pretty girl, uh . . ."

The doctor's voice faded into quiet confusion.

Lucas reached out and took the weapon from his father while aiming a look of bewildered annoyance at Adele.

"Where is Maxine?"

Edmund shuffled to his right and glanced back at Adele, hoping she would be able to answer.

"She was on the ferry when you called and was late getting back. Your dad took a walk, and I found him and brought him back and ended up staying the night here."

The sheriff lifted his chin upward as he processed what he had been told.

"Oh, I see. Well, thank you, Adele, for watching him for me. I appreciate it. Since you're already here, we should talk—privately. I have some information you should know about."

Adele realized how tired the sheriff appeared. His uniform was badly wrinkled, indicating it had been slept in, and dark circles had taken up residence underneath his eyes.

Lucas looked at his father.

"Dad, can you wait in the kitchen? I need to speak to Adele for a bit. We'll be in your study."

"I was going to show her the roses, but OK, if it's important."

Lucas placed a hand on his father's shoulder.

"Yes, it's important, Dad. Thank you."

Adele followed the sheriff back into the study, where he proceeded to carefully return the gun onto its mount above the file cabinet. He motioned toward a small leather couch that sat against the wall kitty-corner from his father's desk.

"Please, have a seat."

The door was closed. Lucas sat down behind the desk and began to rub his temples. When he spoke, it was in the voice of a man suddenly aged far beyond his years.

"The DNA test was a match. The remains in the crab pot came from the same person whose brush you gave to me."

Adele was about to speak, but Lucas held up his hand.

"No, I'm not done, Adele. You're going to tell me who that brush belonged to, and then you're going to tell me the name of the person who gave it to you. I need you to listen very carefully. I'm not asking. I'm *telling* you to give me the names—right now."

Adele didn't hesitate to deliver the first part of the sheriff's request. She wanted to watch Lucas's reaction when he heard the name spoken aloud.

"Her name was Nadia Orlov."

The sheriff visibly flinched.

"The hostess at the Crow's Nest?"

Adele wondered if Lucas would lie or tell her the truth.

"That's right. You know her?"

Lucas nodded slowly.

"I spoke with her briefly at her work. Well, she was off work but drinking in the lounge. I suspected she was underage. I gave her a verbal warning and escorted her partway home on foot. She had an apartment just a few of blocks away."

"And that's the only interaction you ever had with her?"

The sheriff's eyes lifted upward toward the ceiling as he contemplated Adele's words.

"So, it was Nadia Orlov's roommate who gave you that brush?"

"Yes. And don't ask me where she is, because I have no idea."

Lucas bit down on his lower lip.

"Adele, I'm sure I don't need to tell you how this looks. I'm no longer merely investigating this murder case. I just became a primary suspect."

"I know."

Even as she spoke the words, Adele also reminded herself of something very important.

He didn't lie to me. Lucas told the truth.

The sheriff's shoulders slumped. He appeared lost, uncertain, a weary traveler upon a path leading to a potentially dangerous destination. The study was silent for nearly a minute, though it felt far longer as both Lucas and Adele said nothing. Finally, the sheriff began to nod. He had made a decision.

"OK, this thing needs to be done aboveboard. I won't allow even a whiff of abuse of power."

Adele watched as Lucas took out his cell phone.

"Gunther, I need you in my office ASAP. It has to do with the investigation into the remains near Ripple Island. I'm placing myself on temporary leave until the investigation is completed. You'll be acting sheriff during that time. That's right. I'll explain everything when I see you later today. Please update Deputy Smith for me. OK. Thank you."

Adele's voice made clear how stunned she was.

"You're taking yourself off the case?"

"Yeah, I have to. What if I was one of the last people to see Nadia Orlov alive? I can't be involved knowing that is a possibility. I'm supposed to be rebuilding the integrity of the sheriff's office, not further destroying it."

The sheriff's eyes bore into Adele.

"You *will* give me the name of that roommate, though."

"I told you, I don't know where she is."

"Give me a name, and I'll have my deputies start the process of locating her. You have to know that the roommate is a suspect in this murder investigation as well. Besides, we'll get the name one way or another. We can interview coworkers, the landlord, it's just a matter of helping us save time or choosing to be uncooperative."

Adele knew Lucas was right about how easy it would be for him to find out that Paula Mendoza was Nadia's roommate. It was only a matter of time. She decided to use her cooperation as leverage to get her own answers from him.

"I'll give you the name of the roommate if you promise to answer a couple of questions for me."

The sheriff resumed rubbing his temples.

"Sure."

Adele pointed at the Colt 45.

"When is the last time you fired that gun?"

Lucas glanced at the revolver and then grunted, realizing the true intent of the question.

"Yeah, it fires the same caliber of bullet that hit your car. I took out the firing pin years ago, when my dad first showed signs of his illness. His doctor said depression could become a problem for him, so having a gun down here in his study seemed like a bad idea. Without the firing pin, it's just a realistic-looking toy. I also got rid of the bullets when I took the pin out. That weapon hasn't been fired for a long time, Adele, and I assure you, it wasn't what was used on your vehicle."

Adele stared into the sheriff's eyes to try to determine if any deception resided within them. Lucas in turn gave a quick shrug of his broad shoulders.

"And your second question?"

"Your dad started to tell me what happened between you and Ophelia Norris shortly before you left for college. I want you to tell me the rest."

Lucas went limp in the chair as he ran a hand through his unwashed hair. He didn't have the strength to put up a fight on the subject of Ophelia Norris anymore.

"OK, fine. It's actually related to that gun there. Ophelia was arguing with my mother. They hated each other. Ophelia blamed my mom for repeatedly telling me to take advantage of my opportunities after high school, opportunities that meant I might leave the state to play football somewhere else. Ophelia didn't have those same opportunities. Her family's fishing business was struggling badly. They didn't have the money to send her to college out of state. They used to run two or three boats all year long. Last I heard, there was just one left that was still in service, though I don't think she even fishes anymore. I'm sure you saw some of the boats rotting in her yard."

Adele nodded.

"Yeah, I did."

Lucas pointed at the Colt 45.

"Well, anyways, Ophelia had a temper. Her whole family did. She had actually started getting counseling from my dad for it. Ophelia had come over to try and talk me out of accepting the full-ride offer from North Alabama, and Mom lit into her. My mother hardly ever cursed, but on that day she was ripping into Ophelia, telling her to get the hell out and to leave me alone. Ophelia lost it. She ran down the hallway into this study and grabbed the gun, came back out, and pointed it right at my chest. Mom jumped in front of me and Ophelia pulled the trigger. It wasn't loaded, but Ophelia didn't know. At that moment, she was willing to kill my mother."

Lucas brought his hands together and folded them tightly on the desk in front of him.

"To this day, I don't fully recall what happened after that. Mom later told me I pushed her out of the way so I could stand in front of Ophelia. I ripped the gun out of her hand and then hit her in the face so hard she slammed backwards against the door frame and collapsed onto the floor at my feet. I do remember looking down at her and not feeling anything but hate. For a few seconds, I really did want her dead. If Ophelia had hurt my mother, I would have killed her."

Lucas opened his hands and stared at them.

"Mom called my dad at work and told him what happened. He rushed home and treated Ophelia's injury. She had a black eye and a large bump on the back of her head. He checked her for a concussion, and then Dad did what he always would do."

"What was that?"

Lucas grimaced.

"The right thing. He called the sheriff directly. The sheriff arrived here, and after hearing my mother's side of things told Ophelia she was lucky I hadn't done more to hurt her. He said she deserved more and if it had been him in his house, she would have gotten it. And that was it. No report was written up on the incident, like it never happened.

"The sheriff drove Ophelia home, told her parents what she did, what I did, and said it was best for all concerned if no more was said about it. Of course, people saw Ophelia's face, the bruising, and soon after the rumors started. I left for college and then later went into the military, while she stayed here on the island even after her family all left. We haven't spoken more than a few words to each other in passing ever since, though I see her around. She rides that bike of hers everywhere."

Adele pushed herself up off the couch.

"Thank you for doing what you just did, Lucas."

The sheriff arched a brow.

"What was that?"

"The right thing—you told me the truth."

Lucas stood up from behind the desk.

"What are you going to do now?"

Adele's eyes gave off a determined gleam.

"I'm going to do the right thing, too."

The sheriff cocked his head.

"And what is that?"

Adele's voice was absent doubt, a thing of tenacious certainty that left Lucas looking at her with unabashed admiration.

"I'm going to find out who murdered Nadia Orlov."

22.

Adele didn't realize her phone's battery was dead until she attempted to check her messages while sitting in her car after leaving Lucas's home. She made the drive back to Roche Harbor and returned to her sailboat, where she promptly plugged the phone into its charger.

Minutes later, she was able to confirm that Roland had in fact followed through on his promise to send her the download link for the surveillance video showing the brief exchange between Lucas Pine and Nadia Orlov.

While the file was downloading, Adele took a quick shower and put on the only clean clothes she had left: a pair of green khaki pants and a black-and-red Ramones T-shirt. She sat down with her phone at the small table adjacent to the boat's galley area and proceeded to watch the video several more times, looking for anything she might have missed earlier. It was during the fifth viewing that she was interrupted by a knock from outside against the side of the sailboat.

"Ms. Plank?"

Adele stood up, opened the door, and looked out to see who it was.

Phillip Ozere stood on the dock with his hands clasped behind him. He didn't appear overly pleased to find himself standing under the midday sun, especially given he was dressed in black slacks and a black dress shirt, attire not conducive to the eighty-plus degree summer weather.

"Apologies for the interruption, Ms. Plank."

Adele was in fact annoyed at having her investigative work halted by the surprise visit from Tilda's hotel manager and didn't bother with trying to hide it.

"What is it, Phillip?"

"Ms. Ashland requests your presence for dinner on Saturday at the hotel—nine p.m."

Adele groaned, uncertain if she would have the time to spare while also wanting to stay on good terms with the unpredictable hotel owner.

"I'll do my best to make it but no guarantees."

Phillip lifted his chin upward and gave a tight-lipped smile.

"Very good, Ms. Plank, I'll let Ms. Ashland know to expect you at nine."

Adele watched Phillip's stiff-postured departure, somewhat amused by how out of place he appeared among the far more casual summer boating crowd he was forced to navigate through on his way back to the hotel.

She returned to the interior of the sailboat and her intention to make good on the promise to solve the murder of Nadia Orlov. It was nearly twenty minutes later that Adele squinted at something she noticed in the video footage. The object was partially hidden both by distance and shadow, but after replaying the video over and over again, Adele was certain of what she saw.

There was Lucas speaking to Nadia, who then laughed at something he said, and shortly thereafter they left the lounge together. What appeared to be a bicycle helmet remained visible atop a table in the background until a group of four stood at the bar for a short time, hiding it from the surveillance camera's view. When the four then left, the helmet was no longer there.

Adele scribbled her thoughts down on the mental paper of her mind in an effort to determine if the once-disparate pieces of Nadia Orlov's murder puzzle were finally falling into place.

There was one more critical bit of evidence that yet remained, something Adele knew was necessary to confirm her suspicion.

I have to get back to Friday Harbor.

The walk to her MINI was a blur, Adele's mind completely immersed in the possibility of solving the mystery. It wasn't until she brought out her keys to unlock the driver door that she again had the sense of unseen eyes upon her.

The parking lot was full, with a number of vehicles entering and leaving and pedestrians lining both sides. Adele took a moment to look around hoping to find the source of her discomfort but instead only found the typical summer mass of island tourists happily milling about.

During the drive to Friday Harbor, Adele repeatedly glanced into the rearview mirror for evidence she was being followed, but, again, saw nothing to indicate her paranoia was justified. Without thinking to do so, she began to hum in her head the lyrics to the classic Kinks song devoted to that very subject.

Paranoia, will destroy ya.

After quickly parking her car on a side street, Adele made her way downhill toward the expansive Friday Harbor marina. Where Roche Harbor was unmistakably idyllic, the Friday Harbor marina was a teeming cauldron of both commercial and recreational boating activity and had long been the epicenter of island commerce. It boasted nearly double the slips of its Roche Harbor counterpart, a fact clearly evidenced by the thousands of people who swarmed the vast facility.

Adele jogged down the primary access ramp to the marina docks below. A quick scan of the area indicated the smaller commercial fishing vessels were located to her immediate left on the dock closest to land. It was there that Adele hoped to realize final confirmation of her just-emerged theory on who dumped the body of the young Russian woman into the dark waters surrounding Ripple Island.

As Adele scanned the floating contents of multiple boat slips, a ferry announced its arrival into Friday Harbor with an uproarious blast of its horn that caused a multitude of seagulls to cry out angrily in response. The small vessels were a mismatched exhibit of various colors, conditions, and hull materials. Most were fiberglass, some were aluminum, and a few were of wood-crafted construction.

Despite those differences, each and every one shared a common attribute—a small metal-framed anchor light attached to the stern. That is, until Adele came upon the one boat with its anchor light missing.

I'm not sure. It was no more than twenty feet long. The helm was on the right side, with an open fishing area in the back. Oh, there is something I just remembered. The anchor light, the one you normally see sitting up two or three feet on the stern, was broken off, as if something had hit it.

That was the answer Tilda's mysterious hotel guest had given Adele when she asked him if the boat he had seen the night the body was dumped was older or newer.

Adele found the boat, its name written across the transom in bold black letters.

Resolution.

Adele also discovered a ruddy-cheeked, red-bearded man stepping off that same boat as she stood staring at it. He wore fish gut–stained blue sweatpants and an equally dirty white T-shirt. His large heavily calloused hands were evidence of many years of fishing, pulling pots, and tying dock lines. A dark knit cap was pulled over his head, while his feet were housed in a pair of black rubber boots.

"Can I help you?"

The fisherman's voice was a low rumble, friendly enough though also clearly cautious regarding Adele's intentions.

"Is this your boat?"

The man rose to his full height of nearly six feet and nodded.

"I run it every season I can, if that's what you mean. Why do you ask?"

Adele pointed at the damaged area where the anchor light should have been, trying to sound every bit the harmless tourist.

"What happened there?"

The man gave an indifferent shrug.

"That would be the boat owner's doing. Guess she got a wild bug up her butt to take it out the other day for some reason. First time she's been on it in months. Made a damn mess, too. Must have hooked into a decent-size fish from all the blood she left on the deck for me to clean up. And the broken anchor light, too, of course. I suppose I'll get around to replacing it eventually. I lease it from her for my own fishing business. You ever try and buy your own boat? Damn things are expensive as hell! Let me give you a piece of advice, young lady. Stay in school so you don't end up a poor schmuck like me, buried in fish scum and crab shells for a living."

The fisherman chuckled at his own advice as he removed his skull cap and used it to wipe his forehead.

"Whew, it's a hot one today!"

Adele could feel her heart racing. The puzzle was nearly solved.

"What's the name of the woman you lease the boat from?"

The man scowled, his suspicion returned.

"That's common enough knowledge around here. What's *your* name, anyway?"

"Adele Plank. I work for the newspaper."

The fisherman scratched the red-gray stubble on his cheek and then snapped his fingers together.

"Yeah, I've heard of you! There was that story last year about the writer fella and his wife. Man that was something. That was you, right?"

Adele nodded.

"Yes, that was me."

The man stuffed his hands into the front pockets of his sweatpants and regarded Adele with newfound curiosity.

"Is this about another story?"

Adele realized she had become so anxious for an answer, she had been holding her breath.

"It might be."

The fisherman shrugged.

"Well, hell, like I said, it's common knowledge. There are at least a dozen people up and down this dock alone who could tell you whose vessel this is."

Another ferry horn blast erupted around the Friday Harbor marina. Once the blaring call subsided, Adele was finally given her answer.

"This here is Ophelia Norris's boat."

23.

The Island Gazette

Dark Waters

by Adele Plank

Human nature is a confounding, complex, and sometimes dangerous thing.

This week, that lesson was visited upon our island community with the arrest of longtime resident Ophelia Norris for the horrific murder of nineteen-year-old Nadia Orlov.

Nadia had been a recent arrival to San Juan Islands at the time of her death. She was a young woman who, like so many others who come here, was simply seeking a new beginning. Her coworkers described her as outgoing and quick to laugh at herself, especially her penchant for mispronouncing words due to her still-thick Russian accent.

Nadia Orlov wanted what so many of us do at her age—time to discover ourselves. Instead, what she found was another woman's murderous rage. That promise of time was ripped from Nadia at the hands of a daughter of these islands, a deeply disturbed thing who had long ago lost herself to her own terrible and seemingly uncompromising insecurities.

When Sheriff Lucas Pine arrived at Ophelia Norris's Cattle Point residence, Ophelia offered no defense, no deception, nor any attempts at subterfuge for what she had done. She simply didn't care. Instead, she happily offered herself once again to the man who Ophelia believed now, just as she did long ago, had always been meant for her and her alone. She was trapped in a past that no longer existed and instead chose to embrace a full-on denial of both her present and future.

Nadia Orlov, by tragic happenstance, became in the mind of Ophelia Norris a direct threat to that must-have-again point in time, when a young cheerleader was so happily matched to her quarterback. And in what can only be described as tragic irony, Ophelia then became the murdering criminal matched to her sheriff.

This reporter watched as Sheriff Pine calmly explained to Ophelia Norris the severity of what she had done and the implications it would have upon what remained of her own life. Ophelia was clearly without concern for those implications. Instead, she was entirely enamored within the moment that saw her high school love once again taking an interest in her. The motivation for that interest, the blood on her hands that made that interest necessary, didn't matter.

Whoever Ophelia Norris once was and whatever she might one day have been were entirely lost within the swirling midnight mist of her own insanity. She admitted her crime to the sheriff with cold indifference. The taking of a life Ophelia incorrectly assumed was competing for the affections of Lucas Pine meant nothing, an act that to her was not so much a complication as it was an inconvenience. This community's sheriff was merely doing his job when he made certain to see a young woman returned home safely. That gesture was tragically misinterpreted by the jealous madness of one who had taken to carefully monitoring the comings and goings of Sheriff Pine, and who then mistakenly thought Nadia guilty of wanting a man Ophelia secretly continued to claim as her own.

Two weapons further implicating Ms. Norris for the murder of Nadia Orlov were found in her home. One was a cleaver knife used to hack Nadia's body into pieces so that it could be placed into the crab pot Ophelia then so casually dropped into the waters near Ripple Island, a place she knew well from her time spent exploring these islands as a teenager. The other was a .45-caliber pistol used to shoot at the car of yours truly.

You see, reader, Sheriff Pine informed me that I could very well have met with the same fate as Nadia Orlov if Nadia's murder had been left unsolved. Ophelia's terrible mental sickness would have required it be so. She admitted to watching me from afar speaking with the sheriff on numerous occasions and quite possibly was forming a plan to do something similar to me as what Ophelia had done to Nadia.

A hearing to determine Ophelia Norris's mental competency to stand trial has already been scheduled. Off-the-record sources have indicated it's likely she will be found insane, and given Ms. Norris has already admitted to her crime, there will be no trial. The world around us, such as it is, will move on, just as it inevitably moved on from the life Ophelia wanted toward the life without the high school romance she couldn't comprehend living without. She felt she had lost the life of her choosing so was compelled to take the lives of others.

In that sense, Ophelia Norris, the murderer of Nadia Orlov, had already died years ago. It's just that nobody had bothered to notice.

Inside her tastefully decorated apartment on the top floor of the Roche Harbor Hotel, Tilda Ashland lowered the newspaper so she could peer across the small dining table at one of her two dinner guests.

Though Adele wasn't certain, she thought she saw tears welling up within the hotel owner's normally frigid eyes.

"Unlike so many of your contemporaries, you don't merely regurgitate detail, Adele. You tell the story of what happened without taking one side and willfully pitting it against the other while also keeping the humanity of both sides intact. I appreciate that and am confident others do as well."

Adele knew Tilda's words were, for her, uncommon high praise, just as she also knew Tilda had a natural affinity for wanting to understand Ophelia Norris's plight since it somewhat mirrored her own long descent into mental instability following the mistakenly believed death of her friend Calista Stone. Tilda continued to stare at Adele and then arched an eyebrow.

"You are already well beyond expectation and proving yourself worthy of my trust. I can be a powerful ally for you going forward as you continue to unearth the many as yet untold secrets to be discovered just beneath the beautiful exterior of our islands."

Adele spoke the three words she felt provided the most appropriate response.

"Thank you, Tilda."

The other dinner guest that evening was the bearded stranger who had given Adele the clue of the broken anchor light that ultimately helped lead to Ophelia Norris's arrest. After reading Adele's article he had remained silent, staring down at the largely uneaten portions of glazed pork loin and steamed vegetables on his plate. Then he lifted his head and his abnormally dark eyes bore into Adele.

"With the case solved, you've given my little island back to me. I can return home and so am in your debt."

Adele exchanged a questioning glance with Tilda, who appeared to sense exactly what Adele was thinking, given the amused glint in Tilda's eyes.

The stranger picked up on Adele's uncertainty as well. He folded his arms across the blue blazer he wore and gave his dinner host a knowing wink.

"Because you have seen me, you have believed; blessed are those who have not seen and yet have believed."

Tilda issued a brief laugh as she reached across the table and gave Adele's forearm a gentle squeeze.

"It's a verse from the Bible. If anyone suffers a God complex, it would be him!"

The man rested his elbows on the table and folded his hands under his chin.

"Ms. Plank, why haven't you come right out and asked me who I am?"

"Because I don't have time for games. I don't want to get caught up in your delusion."

Tilda sat mesmerized by the exchange between her guests. The man straightened his shoulders. His mouth, almost completely hidden within the thick, prickly forest of his beard, broke apart into a wide, toothy smile.

"My delusion, you say? This from someone who helped free a poor woman from a twenty-seven-year prison sentence in the dark, dank basement of a father and son both gone mad and who just recently solved a murder carried out by a wretched young woman trapped in the pretend world of her own past? What you dismiss as delusion, I call my own reality, Ms. Plank. As you should have already come to realize, there is no limit to the fantastical and frightening possibilities contained within the temporary vessel of our own lives—especially here among these islands where all things are seemingly possible."

The man slowly lowered his hands from beneath his chin and rested them atop the white silk tablecloth that covered the dining table.

"I am going to extend an invitation that you follow me on my return trip to my home on Ripple Island. Allow me to convince you of who I was so that you can then better know me for who I am."

"Why does it matter? Why do you want my approval?"

The man stroked his beard as he pondered the question.

"Hmmm, perhaps it is simply that I respect you, Adele. Tilda said she would help you to discover the many as yet untold secrets contained within the mist of our beloved corner of the world. It would please me greatly to be counted among the first such secrets you are to discover."

The sound of a clock's chime echoed within the otherwise silent residence and was joined by the cheerful revelry of laughing boaters standing somewhere outside the hotel. Adele shrugged.

"A boat trip to Ripple Island, huh? Sure, why not? And I suppose you're a "leave at the crack of dawn" kind of guy, aren't you?"

The man's answer was accompanied by a smiling nod.

"That I am, Ms. Plank. That I am."

Tilda refilled all three wine glasses and then held her own high.

"A toast, then, to long-kept secrets and those capable and willing enough to realize them."

The glasses clinked together over the table. The sound made by their temporary union was a cheerful starting note for what Adele sensed to be a new beginning for her, one that would include, as it so often had for her over the past year, a trip across the pristine saltwater canvas of the San Juan Islands.

24.

Left early. See you there.

That was the note Adele discovered stuck to the side of her sailboat the following morning. The stranger had already made good on his return to Ripple Island with the belief she would soon follow.

Adele looked down at Decklan Stone's runabout. It would be her first time driving a boat entirely on her own. She scanned the passage to the north beyond the Roche Harbor marina and found the waters relatively calm with a slight breeze coming in from the northeast. It was just past 7:00 a.m. The resort was not yet fully awake, and boat traffic into and out of the marina was minimal. After checking to make certain there was enough fuel to get her to Ripple Island and back, Adele slipped into a life vest, started the small four-stroke outboard, untied from the dock, and pointed the runabout toward the entrance to Roche Harbor and the waters of Spieden Channel beyond. A sport fisherman in a small aluminum-hulled vessel sped into the harbor, slowed down, and gave Adele a cheerful wave. Adele waved back. She felt as if she was now truly among them, the island folk of the San Juans.

The dark glistening form of a playful seal poked its head up just a few yards away to peer at Adele as if to give her a greeting similar to that of the passing fisherman's. With a delighted smile, Adele waved at the seal as well and then pushed the throttle control forward. Whatever early morning fatigue she might have had quickly dissipated under the onslaught of sea wind on her face.

Adele recalled a quote from the professional surfer Bethany Hamilton and realized that for the first time she fully grasped its meaning:

"Being out there in the ocean, God's creation, it's like a gift He has given us to enjoy."

For though Adele had journeyed these same waters before, to be seated behind the wheel of the runabout on her own and captaining the course of her immediate future was undeniably different.

Adele moved past the heavily forested shores of Pearl Island to her left and the dark rock shoal that was Barrier Island to her right on her way toward the high grass-swept cliffs of Spieden Island that dominated the landscape on the opposite side of the channel. The shimmering smooth waters of Roche Harbor gave way to the more common chop of the waters beyond the marina.

Adele bumped the runabout's speed up until its bow temporarily lifted before it settled back down as the little vessel went on plane, allowing it to skim across the waves, providing both speed and relative comfort as it did so.

Soon, Adele reached the northern tip of Spieden Island, and then she sped off across New Channel and the southern end of John's Island, where Ripple Island was located. The chop on the south side of Spieden was replaced by slow-moving rolling waves on the island's north side, forcing Adele to slow her speed and allow the runabout to climb the crest of each roller, descend it, and then repeat the process as the next roller arrived.

Initially, Adele found herself gripping tight to the steering wheel as she felt herself lifted and then plunged downward while the little boat traversed each wave, but before long she grew accustomed to the sensation and learned to trust the runabout's ability to continue pushing forward.

Adele spotted a forty-foot trawler a few hundred yards off her starboard side and the large wake the much bigger vessel was creating. She further slowed her speed and turned the wheel to the right, making certain to point the runabout's bow directly into the oncoming wake-produced wave, knowing she didn't want to have the wave directly impact the side of the small boat. The trawler's captain, an older man in a red baseball cap, smiled and waved, seemingly certain Adele was up to the task of navigating the temporarily challenging waters created by his ship's passing.

It was a confidence Adele didn't entirely share.

Suddenly, it felt as if the runabout's bow was slammed by the palm of a large hand and then shoved upward. Adele felt herself pushed back into her seat. The motor behind her gave off a water-choked gurgling sound as the top of the transom kissed the sea. And then just as quickly, the runabout corrected itself, crested the wave, and moved on.

"Hah!"

A seagull flying overhead glanced down at Adele's triumphant shout as she pushed the throttle lever forward again. With the trawler's wake behind her, Adele's confidence was fully returned. She spotted Ripple Island ahead and estimated she would be nearing its hidden, inhospitable shores within a few minutes.

That time allowed Adele a moment to evaluate the man responsible for her latest journey by boat. Tilda Ashland's strange bearded acquaintance had extended an invitation to the island he called home but that Adele still believed was likely no more than an extension of the man's delusion that he was the long-deceased actor, Brixton Bannister.

Why Tilda was so willing to entertain that same delusion left Adele more confused. Tilda assured Adele that her guest wasn't dangerous and that a journey with him to Ripple Island would not only prove safe, but also more enlightening than she likely could imagine. Tilda's assurances left Adele wondering if the stranger really could be Brixton Bannister. Neither the actor's plane he was piloting nor his body were ever found. Could such a deception be possible?

Adele's head turned in the direction of the roar of a vessel approaching from behind. She saw the familiar blue hull and the even more familiar face of Sergei behind the wheel. His mouth was a grim slash as he glared across the diminishing distance of water between them. Adele knew there was no hope of escape. Sergei's boat was much too fast.

The Russian's cruiser pulled up even to Adele's runabout and remained there sixty yards off her starboard side. Each locked eyes on the other. Adele refused to be the first to look away, determined to make certain Sergei knew she would not be intimidated by him. That message was received. The moment lasted no more than a few seconds and though words were not spoken, much was communicated between the two.

The Russian gave her a tight-lipped sneer before speeding off toward the Canadian border.

Adele sensed it was inevitable their paths would cross again. Whatever business Roland Soros had with the Russian, Adele intended to bring it to light. Sergei knew this to be true—and he feared it, just as he had come to fear Adele and her ability to discover the truth.

Adele was once again alone as she entered the reef-strewn waters around Ripple Island. She located the hidden cove and saw the dilapidated skiff she had first spotted in Roche Harbor already pulled up onto the shore and tied to the smooth-trunked shrub both she and Avery had investigated days earlier.

Adele blinked several times as she studied the now clean-shaved man standing casually near the skiff. He wore loose-fitting tan khakis rolled up nearly to the top of his calves, a gray-striped sweater, and a pair of scuffed leather fisherman sandals. His long brown-and-silver-streaked hair was tied back from a lean face complemented by prominent cheekbones and a hard-edged square jaw.

I know that face. It's really him!

Brixton Bannister didn't smile. His flinty eyes betrayed to Adele the uncertainty he felt over whether or not he should be revealing his secret to the young journalist. Adele had by then stood up in the runabout and was staring at the actor with her mouth half-open, still unable to believe the incomprehensible sight of the alleged dead man who stood before her.

The actor waded knee-high into the water and called out for Adele to throw him the bowline and to remember to tilt up the outboard prior to beaching the runabout. Adele hesitated for several seconds before shaking off her stunned confusion. She threw the rope and tilted the outboard and then waited as Brixton pulled the little boat up onto the shore and tied if off to the same shrub that held his skiff in place.

"Ms. Plank, before I show you anything more, I need your assurance this is a secret you intend to keep for as long as I require. If you agree, then I will promise you that someday this story *will* be yours to tell, if you so choose."

Adele tried to avoid staring at the actor but found she was unable. Instead, she merely shook her head in wide-eyed disbelief.

"Why me?"

The actor stuffed his hands into the loose pockets of his pants, looked up into the sun-drenched morning sky, and took a long, deep breath.

"You already count a renowned writer among your closest friends, why not an actor as well? And who knows what future mysteries might someday reveal themselves to you? Tilda intends to help you discover the secrets of these islands. I would like to do the same. I am a man of very few friends. I thought perhaps you might be willing to be counted among those few."

Adele realized Brixton Bannister, the iconic actor of an era since past, was a very lonely man. He wanted friendship, namely a friend who could be trusted with the great secret that was his ongoing existence among the world of the living.

With a smile and a nod, Adele extended her hand.

"Call me Adele."

Brixton paused as his dark eyes took in Adele's form, seeming to look not so much at her as into her in an attempt to determine her truth. Once he thought that truth confirmed, he took Adele's hand into his own.

Though she had no way of knowing it then, that handshake was the beginning of not merely a happenstance acquaintance, but also a remarkable friendship that would rival the one Adele already enjoyed with the writer Decklan Stone.

You already count a renowned writer among your closest friends, why not an actor as well?

Adele had taken note of Brixton Bannister's words, but it would be some time yet before she would fully understand them or the bind between otherwise disparate lives that Adele herself would provide.

A writer.

An actor.

Adele couldn't help but wonder who might be next.

Over the next hour, Brixton proudly showed Adele the long-forgotten film set that had been his home for much of the last decade. It was a cave originally carved over millennia by the fingers of wind, waves, and time that had been discovered by a now-deceased Hollywood director during a sailing trip through the islands many years ago. That same director returned to Ripple Island with the intention of shooting a film in which the production's main character, played by Brixton Bannister, would reside on the island.

Months were spent, accompanied by over two million dollars, further carving out the cave and turning it into a self-sufficient film set boasting fine furnishings, a water system, and a secret entrance. Just three weeks into filming saw Brixton and the director at each other's throats. Soon after, studio executives halted production altogether due to enormous cost overruns and too little actual film footage created.

After more than twenty years in the business, and tens of millions of dollars in earnings, the actor suffered from deep disenchantment over his chosen craft, thinking himself a prisoner within the part of Brixton Bannister, a Hollywood creation who had little in common with the man he actually desired to be.

The utter disaster of his final project was what pushed the film star into finally doing the seemingly unthinkable. Brixton Bannister the star was put to death so that Brixton the man might live.

Though Brixton didn't say, and Adele didn't ask, the reporter was certain Tilda Ashland helped to facilitate the deception of the actor's supposed demise. What would motivate the hotel owner to do so remained unknown, but Adele thought perhaps someday Tilda might reveal her side of that most peculiar tale.

Brixton showed Adele his surprisingly vast collection of books kept on shelves cut out from the cave's rocky interior as well as the sink connected to a long siphon that gathered rainwater from outside and delivered it inside for use. A large, ornately framed bed sat at the back of the cave. Over the dark oak headboard was a black iron candelabra. The actor would often read in bed by its candlelight.

"Once production was halted, this place was abandoned by the film crew and soon forgotten. When I returned after having staged my death, I found it just as I remembered. Everything was in its place, including the hidden passage to gain entrance."

The hidden passage was an ingenious path to the cave's opening that was only revealed during particularly low tides, and even then it required someone to be seeking such an opening at that given time. During her visit with Avery to the island, Adele had been standing on the other side of the cave without knowing it was there. The tide was in, the path covered, and the actor's home hidden by a fake Hollywood-produced thicket of brush.

The cave's floor was planked hardwood attached to beams that kept it several inches off the sand and stone bottom. A tall LED lantern stood in the middle of the space, providing ample light. Brixton explained how he had in recent years taken to snorkeling around the various tide pools that surrounded the little island and spearing the occasional fish for a meal. A stack of milk crates inside the cave acted as a makeshift pantry, where boxes of energy bars and canned drinks were kept.

"I have a set of clothes I keep at Tilda's hotel, and I go there once a month for supplies, a hot shower, and a proper meal. Other than that, this is where I live. It stays cool in the summer and reasonably warm in the winter. There's a shallow pool with a strong tidal change on the island's northern side where I take care of my toiletries. Each outgoing tide flushes out to sea, and I never have to worry about jiggling the handle."

The actor's attempt at a joke fell flat. He winced and shook his head as an apology for his brief comedic performance.

"I spent years being paid millions of dollars for being told what to say only to realize I don't have much talent for coming up with my own words."

With the initial wonder of the hidden space having passed, Adele looked around and noted how small the cave actually was.

"How much longer do you intend to live out here, Brixton?"

The actor grinned. It was a question he had asked himself many, many times, but its answer had yet to reveal itself.

"As long as it takes."

Brixton escorted Adele back to the beach where the runabout waited. On the way, he pointed to a group of black porpoises swimming slowly off the little island's eastern shore. Their dark backs shimmered in the sun as the mammals rolled across the water accompanied by loud sneezing sounds when they exhaled shots of air before taking another breath.

"They come by here at about this time nearly every day to say hello. There used to be nine of them, but I think one of the grandparents died last winter."

Adele and Brixton stood side by side, watching the porpoise family's graceful journey into deeper waters.

"There is pleasure in the pathless woods, there is rapture in the lonely shore, there is society where none intrudes, by the deep sea, and music in its roar; I love not Man the less, but Nature more."

The actor looked down at Adele and appeared somewhat embarrassed at having spoken the words.

"It's Lord Byron. I learned the line for a play long ago when I could still be considered an artist, before celebrity replaced art with greed and self-interest."

Adele found the link between Byron and Brixton most appropriate.

"Byron despised society and all its rules, and in the final years of his young life, he felt trapped by an image that had almost completely overtaken the man."

Brixton grunted.

"Indeed. And bravo on your knowledge of Byron!"

The actor helped Adele into the runabout and then stood on the beach holding the bowline in his hands. He looked just as nervous and uncertain as when Adele had first arrived earlier that morning, though this time it wasn't because he feared she might reveal his secret, but rather that she would leave and never come back.

"You're welcome to stop here any time, Adele. Or check in with Tilda, and she can let you know when I'm to be at the hotel."

Adele's smile was gentle reassurance and was followed by words that intended to do the same.

"I'll see you again soon, Brixton. Until then, be careful out here."

Brixton pushed the boat backward into the water and threw her the bowline.

"I will. Thank you."

After pointing the runabout toward the narrow opening between the reef rocks, Adele looked behind her and saw the actor still standing on the beach watching her departure. Once past the rocks and in open water, Adele looked back again.

The beach was empty.

With her hand resting on the throttle, Adele scanned the sea that lay before her while pondering the stunning story she had just left behind. Adele had given Brixton Bannister her word. The actor's secret would remain untold.

She pushed down on the throttle. The engine growled its approval. The bow lifted and then quickly settled as the water sped past, whispering to Adele of yet more secrets and mysteries awaiting her discovery.

EPILOGUE

One week later . . .

Adele stood in front of the floor-length mirror and took a moment to evaluate the young woman staring back at her as she pondered the journey of the past year.

So much had changed.

Her brown hair was now cut short, a somewhat businesslike, slightly curled bob that framed her leaner face. The act of cutting some of her hair was as much a symbolic gesture of removing the last vestiges of her former insecurities as it was an appeal to fashion. She felt tougher, more confident, and she wanted to look the part.

Adele tightened the blue belt around her waist and then rolled her head from side to side, making certain to remain loose, relaxed, and ready for the test to come.

The walk from the locker room to the almost empty gymnasium was a short one. Sensei Rob stood in the middle of the Bellingham University gym floor, holding the board in his hands. The martial arts instructor avoided looking into the eyes of his student as if to imply his presence had become as inconsequential as that of the board. Each was merely a marker upon the path of Adele's ongoing physical and spiritual improvement.

Adele glanced at the two men watching her from their place on the opposite side of the gym. Lucas Pine wore a denim jacket, red T-shirt, and blue jeans, while Roland Soros was adorned in a decidedly more eccentric ensemble that boasted a custom-fitted cream-colored sport jacket, dark-blue dress shirt, red tie, and red slacks. Both had requested they be allowed to go with Adele to Bellingham to watch her earn her purple belt.

Roland gave Adele an encouraging smile accompanied by a thumbs-up. Lucas wasn't nearly so demonstrative. His eyes narrowed, followed by a short nod of his head. Two very different men, both vying for the attention of a woman not yet certain either was a choice she cared to pursue beyond friendship. Lucas was busy with his role as San Juan County sheriff and as caregiver to his ill father, while Roland represented the even greater unknown of a millionaire businessman who, however well-intentioned he suggested his motivations to be, had ties to at least one likely criminal.

Sensei Rob acknowledged Adele's presence with a short bow, which she then returned. She closed her eyes briefly, took a deep breath, and made a fist.

Her eyes reopened to find the board held directly in front of her, its smooth light-colored surface representing the weakness and uncertainty that had plagued Adele in the months that followed her graduation from college.

The young reporter's jaw tightened as Sensei Rob quietly repeated the very same advice he had given her the last time she had tried and failed to break the board.

"You don't hit *at* it, you hit *through* it."

Adele's eyes flared in defiance at the barrier before her. She was determined to be the captain of her own destiny regardless how troubled the waters of her life might yet prove.

With a snarling shout, Adele didn't merely hit the board.

She obliterated it.

With a crack that echoed throughout the cathedral-like expanse of the gymnasium, the wood exploded in fragments between Sensei Rob's hands. He gave Adele a second bow. This one was much deeper than the first, a show of respect for her accomplishment.

Adele looked over to see Roland clapping. The sheriff shook his head in disbelief and had a wide grin covering his face. Lucas's smile was only half as wide, but his eyes were lit with equally warm approval.

Both men were impressed not only by what Adele had done, but also by the powerful and determined manner in which she had done it.

"You don't seem surprised."

Sensei Rob's voice was calm, measured, and reassuring.

"No, I am not surprised, Adele. It was clear the moment you stepped onto this floor that you were ready. You're different now."

Adele's brows drew together.

"Different? Different how?"

The tae kwon do instructor held up the two broken pieces of board in his hands.

"In every way, you are stronger—*much* stronger."

Adele stood still as Sensei Rob removed the blue belt from around her dobok and carefully replaced it with a purple one. Once that was completed, he stepped back and issued a proud smile.

"Congratulations. So, tell me, where do you intend to go from here?"

It was the very question that not so long ago had been the source of such painful uncertainty in Adele's life. That uncertainty was all but gone, broken apart much like the board that was her most recent test. Adele was at that moment prepared to fully and completely accept Delroy's gift.

She looked at Lucas and Roland as they stood patiently waiting and thought of the islands and their blue-green waters that even then beckoned for her return. She saw, as well, the faces of Tilda, Avery, Bess, Suze, Brixton, and others, a multitude of varied personalities as unique as the land-and-water landscape that surrounded them. There was so much more to learn, so many more mysteries to reveal, and so many more stories to tell. With a faint, upturned hint of a smile, Adele gave her answer.

"I'm going home."

———

ABOUT THE AUTHOR

D.W. Ulsterman is the writer of the Kindle Scout-winning San Juan Islands Mystery & Romance series published by Kindle Press as well as the #1 bestselling and USA Today-featured family drama, *The Irish Cowboy*.

He lives with his wife of 25 years in the Pacific Northwest. During the summer months you can find them navigating the waters of their beloved San Juan Islands. He is the father of two grown children and is also best friends with Dublin the Dobe.

Made in the USA
Monee, IL
30 March 2023